DARKNESS WHISPERS

DARKNESS
WHISPERS

BY

RICHARD CHIZMAR

AND

BRIAN JAMES FREEMAN

JOURNALSTONE
YOUR LINK TO ARTIST TALENT

JournalStone books may be ordered through booksellers
or by contacting:
JournalStone
www.journalstone.com

ISBN: 978-1-945373-87-9 (sc)
ISBN: 978-1-945373-88-6 (ebook)

JournalStone rev. date: June 16, 2017

Library of Congress Control Number: 2017942711

Printed in the United States of America
2nd Edition

Cover Design: Jon Malfi
Image Credit: Elderlemon Design
Interior Artwork copyright © 2016 by Jill Bauman
Interior Design copyright © 2016 by Desert Isle Design, LLC

Someone has to die in order that the rest of us should value life more.

—*Virginia Woolf*

No one can confidently say that he will still be living tomorrow.

—*Euripides*

Because I could not stop for death,
He kindly stopped for me;
The carriage held but just ourselves and immortality.

—*Emily Dickinson*

for Ed Gorman
from two grateful friends

1.

THE FIRST GOLDEN RAYS OF dawn were peeking over the mountain ridge to the east, although this was Western Pennsylvania, so only the locals considered those mountains to actually be mountains. In Colorado, they would be foothills. In Nepal and Tibet, they'd be speed bumps at best.

The old man walking along the twisting country road had been to all of those places and many others, and he found people's incessant desire to center the universe around their own limited range of knowledge and experience to be both amusing and disgusting, depending on the day and his mood.

If anyone happened to drive past the old man, they might think he was a traveler from another time, which was nearly the truth but not exactly right either. He wore a smart black suit and a black Fedora hat with a white band of Petersham. He carried an intricately carved cane made of antique wood and a silver grip, but he didn't limp.

The old man stopped at a wooden sign posted near the shoulder of the road, kicking some loose gravel with his neatly polished shoes. He removed a pair of delicate glasses from the silk lined pocket inside his suit jacket, placed the glasses on his slightly crooked nose, and blinked to align his eyes.

"Welcome to Windbrook, Pennsylvania!" he read, emphasizing the state's name as the exclamation point dictated. "Population, 2,314. PA's Friendliest Small Town!"

The old man returned his glasses to their pocket and resumed walking west.

"Well, we'll just see about that," he said, smiling. The old man picked up his pace and started to whistle.

Behind him, the mountains were alive with the first touch of morning light. The trees glowed like they were on fire.

2.

FURTHER DOWN THE ROAD, THE opening moments of a beautiful April morning crept toward the Skullkin Valley, but most of the residents of Windbrook were still asleep and didn't notice or didn't care. Even the few chronic insomniacs were slumbering. Such was life in a tranquil small town in the middle of nowhere.

It would be another half-hour until Joe Thompson made his way around the community tossing the *Pittsburgh Post-Gazette* from the window of his vintage station wagon. Joe only had one set of clothes, so he didn't roll out of bed until he heard Jason Sinclair's delivery truck approaching with four hundred copies of the day's newspaper.

Earl Duberstein's widow, Betty, might be awake, but she would stick to her hard and fast rule of staying under the covers until daylight kissed her windows. Her mother had said there was no need to burn the kerosene just to make breakfast a few minutes sooner, and Betty felt confident the logic was sound when applied to the PP&L electric bill, too.

Even Carl Reynolds, the town librarian, who used to greet each sunrise with a cup of steaming coffee and a good book in his reading chair by the bay window, remained snug and still under the covers. Carl was nearing seventy, and those early days had simply passed him by. Now, he took his time most mornings, sleeping in until nine or so, and grabbing a quick breakfast sandwich at the Windbrook Diner on his walk across town to open the library doors by ten o'clock.

Bill Smith was busy cleaning and prepping his kitchen at the Windbrook Diner, but he was only half awake. He had been running this kitchen for better than fifty years, grooving and cooking to classic rock songs on WZOE blaring from his battered radio, and he could do the work in his sleep. Sometimes, he thought maybe he did.

Mildred Lotz, Miss Milly to her middle-school English students, *was* awake this fine April morning—camped out in her bathroom for the past twenty minutes, her stomach upset from too many fudge brownies at last night's bridge club meeting—but she was the exception. And an unhappy one at that.

A little more than two thousand other men, women, and children slept in their homes in the valley, whether those homes were large or small, whether they were well maintained or dusty in the corners, and these people shared one thing in common: their understanding of what life in Windbrook was, what life in Windbrook meant. You could set your watch and warrant to dozens of daily occurrences in the town. Predictability and consistency were the hallmarks of their community's existence.

Windbrook was a no-stoplight town like dozens of others in the western part of Pennsylvania, places that even lifelong residents of the state had never heard of. Nestled in the secluded Skullkin Valley, the residents of Windbrook lived in an isolated world of their own—and they liked it that way.

The nearest town, Glenton, was fifteen miles to the south and when the snow came it might as well be fifteen *hundred* miles considering PennDOT could take a week to plow the lone country road between the two communities.

The valley's stunning landscape was the only real attraction to knowledgeable outsiders and the only reason strangers might be spotted traveling the length of Main Street from one side of town to the other. There were two different state parks to the north, both of which brought campers and fishermen in search of the beautiful, peaceful settings only the lands around Windbrook could offer. Shallow streams bubbled down the rolling hills, slicing through the thousands of acres of thick, dark forest. There were still places in those woods where no man had ever stepped, not once in the history of the world.

Life here was leisurely and idyllic—if you came from Windbrook and accepted the nature of small town life. The bright white bell tower rising from the First Church of Christ was the highest point in town and could be seen from anywhere in the valley. There were Saturday little league baseball games and Sunday church picnics. There were Bingo nights at the firehouse the first Friday of every month and bake sales almost every weekend in front of the grocery store. There was a five-person town council and a mayor, and they always won reelection unopposed. There was a single school building, housing all 134 students this year, grades K through 12. The school had been old when the parents of the current students hadn't even been born.

This was an old-fashioned town where everyone knew everyone else's name and also their business, both personal and professional. Windbrook resembled a Norman Rockwell painting—and again, that was just fine with the townspeople.

On this particularly fine April morning, a gentle breeze rattled the tree branches as the air above the mountains burst to life with the vivid colors of the rising sun, mostly red and orange and some purple, the eternal light burning a path into the crisp blue sky.

The doors of the shops on both sides of Main Street were locked, yet they weren't barred and gated like the stores in larger towns and cities. Soon the proprietors would arrive to unlock those doors, uncover their wares, and sell to their friends, neighbors, and the occasional guest passing through. There were no chains or franchises, not even a McDonald's.

Windbrook was just beginning to awaken for the day, but soon the valley would be buzzing with life. This morning was like thousands of other mornings that had come before it, and all was well in Windbrook, just like usual, just like normal.

Nothing was different. Nothing had changed.

3.

EXCEPT SOMETHING *WAS* DIFFERENT IN Windbrook. Something *had* changed.

Sheriff Benjamin Logan couldn't exactly tell what yet, but something was off. He'd never experienced this nervous electric undercurrent in Windbrook, not as a kid growing up here and not in the decade since he was elected Sheriff, but he *had* felt the sensation before. In Fallujah, Iraq, to be exact, during Operation Phantom Fury. On that scorching summer day, the awareness of something being wrong with the world had grown stronger and stronger for Ben while his unit was clearing a bridge over the Euphrates River, reaching an unnerving level the moment before his leg was filled with shrapnel from an IED. The doctors managed to save his leg, but his time in the Army was done.

Before his deployment Ben had married his high school sweetheart, Jennifer, and she had gotten pregnant with their son, Paul, soon after. Some in town whispered about the timing—there was always plenty of whispering in small towns like Windbrook—but the wedding hadn't been a shotgun affair. Ben and Jennifer had been talking marriage since sophomore year.

When Paul was three, a little sister, Mary, joined him. Ben and Jennifer were only twenty-two and they rarely saw each other while he served overseas, but despite the concerns of their friends and family, and despite the mumblings of the old men drinking coffee in the diner or the glib conversations of the old women baking cookies in the basement of the church, their relative youth and Ben's time away hadn't dampened their love. If anything, it only strengthened it.

Jennifer and the kids had been Ben's reason to keep fighting to live as he was bleeding out on that bridge while another soldier dragged him to safety through the ricocheting bullets of sniper fire. Ben's family had been all the motivation he had needed to beat the timetables for getting back on his feet during his rehab stint in Germany, too. Every time he closed his eyes on those painful and haunting nights, he visualized Jennifer and the kids and the town, exactly as they had been when he'd left, just waiting for him to return home. He clung tightly to this image when the agony became unbearable and he used the memory of home to push himself forward.

Once he actually was home, Ben had indeed found everything to be the way he had expected—nothing different, nothing changed—although the kids had grown leaps and bounds, of course. Still, even with that comforting sense of familiarity, he had felt lost and without purpose as the days and weeks passed. He couldn't sleep at night and he found himself taking long walks during the day, searching for something without knowing what it could be.

After a few months of restless puttering around the house and town, and then a month of trying to help with Jennifer's real estate business where he mostly got in the way, his wife encouraged him to join the Sheriff's Department as a deputy, to fill the vacant place inside of him that wanted to help and protect people. He reluctantly applied for the job, was quickly accepted and welcomed to the position, and he had realized how right Jennifer had been as soon as he put on the uniform for the first time. Then, when Leroy Callahaun gave in to his wife's desperate pleas for him to finally retire, Jennifer had urged Ben to run for the job. No one had campaigned against him, and he had been re-elected twice since.

Jennifer and the kids had been the foundation upon which Ben had rebuilt his life, and when he awoke from his frequent nightmares, from the recurring memories of his wounded and dying friends, the mangled and burned corpses of innocent children, and every other horrible thing he had witnessed in the war, Jennifer was always there beside him in the dark, always ready to hold him, always prepared to remind him that life was good, life was normal, the two of them were happy and the kids were safe.

But, now, something was not normal. In fact, something was very wrong.

Sheriff Logan stood outside his patrol car on Main Street, his hand resting above his holster. The old-fashioned street-lights glowed bright and he couldn't entirely remember how he had gotten here. When was the last time he had covered the graveyard shift anyway? The late shift wasn't exactly a common duty for the sheriff, even in a small town where your staff consisted of four deputies and a janitor.

All of the stores were closed, but the lights shone brightly from the windows of the Windbrook Diner, which was to be expected. Bill Smith would be hard at work already. His car was parked in one of the slanted spaces along the tree-lined sidewalk, but the rest of the spaces were empty, which was also to be expected. Everything looked normal. Everything looked okay.

Yet that electric undercurrent was creeping through Sheriff Logan's bones, sending an icy chill across the back of his neck as if cold fingers had caressed him. His hand released the safety strap on his holster without a thought. He had never drawn his weapon in the line of duty as Sheriff, but this felt different. This felt *familiar*. He had fired weapons plenty of times during the war, and this felt too much like a combat situation for reasons he couldn't understand. Something was *terribly* wrong. He could feel the wrongness as much as he could feel the breeze on his sweaty skin.

As he scanned Main Street again, Sheriff Logan spotted an old man in the middle of the road, standing directly on the faded double yellow line. The old man was watching the lawman with a keen interest.

Icy fingers brushing his neck again, Sheriff Logan started walking toward the old man. He didn't recognize him from around town and that bothered the sheriff. What was a stranger doing standing in the middle of Main Street at dawn? Where had he come from? What did he want?

The sheriff had nearly reached the old man—was close enough, in fact, to clearly appreciate the man's odd choice of clothing—when a loud banging sounded from the direction of the diner. Sheriff Logan drew his weapon and spun and

dropped to a knee in one fluid motion. A smiling Bill Smith looked at him from the diner window. He banged one more time on the glass and gave the sheriff a friendly wave.

Sheriff Logan stood and quickly holstered his weapon. Embarrassed, he flipped a distracted wave in the direction of the diner and turned back to the old man.

He was gone.

"What the—?" The sheriff turned in a slow circle, searching the sidewalks and dark pools of shadow hiding beneath each tree.

Nothing. The entire street was silent and still.

Puzzled, he started walking back to his patrol car—and there he was. The old man. Leaning against the hood of the sheriff's cruiser. Waiting for him.

"How the hell—?"

Sheriff Logan approached the old man, instinctively surveying the area again for threats without losing his focus on the subject he was approaching. He raised one hand in a friendly wave while his other hand remained on his hip.

"Hello there," the sheriff said.

The old man grinned, and there was nothing right about that mouth full of gleaming teeth. In fact, nothing at all was right about the old man. Not his expensive suit or his fedora hat or his cane made of wood and silver and engraved with complicated symbols that twisted and wrapped around each other.

Sheriff Logan stopped when he saw that grin. The old man extended his hand to shake and his bony fingers seemed much too long. The old man's slate gray eyes glanced at Sheriff Logan's hands, which hadn't moved to return the greeting.

"If she wasn't six feet under, Betsy Ann Logan would be ashamed of your manners, don't you think?"

"Who are you? How do you know my mother?"

"Oh, Benjamin, if you're already that far behind the game, I don't think I have much to worry about, now do I?"

With that, the old man moved faster than anyone Ben had ever seen, raising the cane and swinging it toward him with dizzying speed. Ben's arm rose automatically to deflect the weapon, and a bright flash of light exploded from the point where his arm and the cane connected.

The light wasn't like the spark of an explosion, but instead a slow wave of brilliant transformation that flowed across the land like lava slinking toward the ocean. In the wake of the light, Sheriff Logan saw a town he barely recognized. Stark fear rose inside him.

The roadway changed from black pavement with a cleanly painted double yellow line to a wasteland of ruined macadam buckled from extreme heat. The antique lampposts were twisted and bent, their lights shattered. The trees were scarred trunks blasted black from a surge of superhot fire. The storefronts were shattered hulks and piles of crumbling brick. The scorched remnants of cars, most of them upside-down on the sidewalks as if tossed by an angry giant, littered the land. There was broken glass and piles of rubble and jagged shards of twisted metal. The air reeked of a slaughterhouse's killing floor that hadn't been cleaned before the building was closed tight for a hot holiday weekend.

There were also thousands of skulls bleached as white as the desert sand, possibly the entire population of Windbrook gathered together in death.

Soaring fires burned in the mountains surrounding the town. The fires were furious, consuming everything they came in contact with, insatiably devouring every last trace of humanity. The black clouds looked almost alive as they streamed to the east and gray ash fell like snow across the devastated land.

"What have you done?" Sheriff Logan asked the old man, their eyes finding each other again in the radiance of the fires surrounding the town.

"What have *I* done?" the old man asked, his tone mocking. "Oh, no, you can't blame me for this, Benjamin. There's no passing the buck here, Mr. War Hero. This is all *your* doing."

4.

BEN AWOKE WITH A JERK, barely holding in his scream. As always Jennifer was already turning on the light on her end-table and reaching for him, still almost entirely asleep but her body moving on autopilot like it had when the kids were babies and they had cried out in the night.

"It's okay," she was saying, running her hand across his arm and then squeezing his hand. "It's okay, baby, it was just a dream."

Ben sat up, breathing heavily and drenched in sweat. Yes, it was a dream. No, it wasn't a dream. This wasn't like the PTSD induced night terrors. This wasn't reliving the past in the same old horrible ways. This was something else, something that didn't feel like a dream even now in the harsh light of his bedroom.

"I'm okay," Ben said, reaching across Jennifer and turning off the light again. He kissed her forehead twice and lay back down. "Go back to sleep, honey, I'm okay."

Jennifer mumbled something and curled up behind Ben, holding him tight to protect him from whatever demons might come searching in the dark, but he had no plans to go back to sleep. Not tonight.

After he was sure his wife was fully asleep, Ben slid out from under her arm and left the bedroom, slowly creeping past the bedrooms of their sleeping children and down the dark stairs. Once he reached the first floor, he turned on every light and made himself a cup of black coffee.

5.

IN THE TWENTY YEARS JASON Sinclair had been driving the battered white delivery truck from Glenton to Windbrook, he could count on one hand the number of times he had seen someone walking along the road between the two towns. Those unfamiliar with the area might have expected him to drive past hunters on their way to their favorite hunting spots from time to time, but the hunters actually stayed far away from the road and they parked in secret places off dirt lanes deep in the woods.

Every morning, Jason delivered four hundred copies of the *Pittsburgh Post-Gazette* to Joe Thompson's shack at the edge of Windbrook, just on the other side of the narrow two lane bridge across the babbling waters of Skullkin Creek, and then he turned around to drive home to Glenton where he lived. Every morning, Jason had this road to himself, with the exception of the occasional herd of deer that might come running from the woods in the dusty first light of the day.

Jason was five miles from Windbrook, bouncing in his seat on the bumpy old road and singing along to some new pop country song on WCOW, The Cow, which even a redneck at heart like Jason thought was an offensive name for a radio station. He loved country songs, though, especially the upbeat ones about having fun with your gal and driving your pick-up truck real fast. The song had just reached the chorus and Jason's voice was cracking to keep up when he rounded one of the dozens of blind curves along his route and he spotted the old man in the black suit standing in the middle of his lane.

"Jesus H. Christ!" Jason yelped as he slammed on the brakes and cut the wheel hard. As the truck skidded on the locked tires, he sensed it starting to tip and pull him toward the side of the road. The truck wanted to roll. In fact, rolling seemed like the best idea in the world right now to the thirty-year-old hunk of steel and ball bearings.

Jason cut the wheel again and the truck slid sideways on the pavement, smoke rising from the tires. Although only seconds could have passed, Jason felt like this turn of events was taking minutes to unfurl before him. He gazed into the old man's calm gray eyes as the truck missed him by mere inches and shuddered to a stop on the wrong side of the faded double yellow line.

Time lurched back to normal and Jason sat there for a moment, gripping the ragged steering wheel so tightly he thought it might break off in his hands. His arms trembled from the adrenaline rushing through his veins. He had experienced plenty of close calls in his time, especially on some of the busier back roads, but this one had been surreal. Where the hell had that old man come from anyway?

"Holy shit, mac!" Jason yelled as he stumbled out of the truck, his hands still shaking. He hurried to make sure he really had missed the crazy old coot and he found that the old man hadn't moved an inch. Hadn't even flinched. "Mister, you could have killed us both! Are you okay? Something wrong with your head or something?"

"Oh, I'm quite all right. How are you on this fine morning, Mr. Sinclair?"

Jason probably should have considered it odd that this old-timer in the fancy suit in the middle of nowhere knew his name, but his memory had been shot ever since he was eighteen years old and he rolled a Winged Sprint Car into the wall at the Greensburg Open Dirt Track. The fireball had been spectacular, according to his friends, but he didn't remember anything about that day, and since then, lots of names and faces came and went from his memory, rising and sinking like a cork in the ocean.

"I'm okay, Mister, you just scared the shit out of me," Jason said, laughing.

"Well, your pants look all right," the old man replied with a sly grin. "Would you mind giving me a lift to town?"

"Sure, happy to," Jason said. He patted at his pockets and frowned. "Now, where did my keys get to?"

"Perhaps you should check the ignition," the old man said, smiling even more broadly as he walked to the passenger side of the truck and hopped on in as if he were twenty instead of... well, whatever age he might be.

Jason opened the driver's side door and, as the old man had suggested, the keys and his Richard Petty key ring were hanging from the ignition. The engine was still running, actually, rumbling the low growl of a working machine ready to get down to business.

"Duh, sorry," Jason said.

"Never apologize, my son," the old man said. "Apologies are for the weak and I can tell you are strong."

Jason shifted the truck into gear and started toward Windbrook. Neither of them said anything for the next few miles, but when they reached Aliquippa Point, a popular scenic pullover spot, the old man asked if Jason could park for a moment. Jason thought the old man's face was looking pretty gray, as gray as his eyes, in fact, and maybe he was going to be sick, so Jason did as he was asked. He didn't want to have to clean old-man puke off the dash.

Instead of making a run for the shoulder to liberate his breakfast, the old man turned to Jason, put one wrinkled hand on his shoulder, and looked him in the eyes. Jason hadn't realized how oddly long the old man's fingers were until this moment, and he also hadn't noticed how the slate hue of the old man's eyes didn't seem to stay gray. The color shifted warmer and then cooler, somehow. Maybe a little green, then a little brown, then a little blue. That was impossible, wasn't it?

"Tell me, Mr. Sinclair, what is your secret dream you share with no one else?"

Jason discovered his mouth was opening to speak even though he didn't know what his answer might be, and he said, "I wish I hadn't busted up my head so bad that I can't remember stuff. I don't want to have to worry about forgetting stuff anymore."

"Oh, that's an easy one, Mr. Sinclair. I can help you with that! For a price, of course."

"A price?"

"Well, more of a favor. You have a choice to make, and if you make the right one, I can assist you in ways you can't even imagine."

The old man grinned again, showing off his impossibly white teeth. Jason didn't like that grin. Somehow it stopped just above the old man's lips, never reaching his eyes. His color-changing eyes were cold and stern.

Yet those colors, those swirling colors, were somehow intoxicating. Jason found himself smiling and nodding along as the man explained what needed to be done.

6.

JENNIFER WAS COOKING BREAKFAST FOR the family, just as she always did, even though she was a thoroughly modern woman with a job, with her own business at that, and plenty of other things to do with her day. She liked cooking, and anyway, Ben's attempts to make bacon never tasted right. How could you screw up bacon? Who knew, but he found a way. Even he admitted it.

Ben was dressed for work, sitting at the table and staring at the front page of the *Pittsburgh Post-Gazette,* but he wasn't reading about the sensational details of the latest political scandal. He was remembering how his nightmare had ended, with the apocalyptic vision of Main Street, with the overwhelming scope of destruction and the piles of skulls and the endless fires for as far as he could see. Unlike most bad dreams, this one hadn't faded away in the bright lights of the kitchen after a hot cup of coffee. Somehow, the memory and the feeling of being trapped by the nightmare had grown even stronger.

Ben stared into nothingness, replaying the events of his dream over and over, while Paul and Mary tapped away at their phones, playing games or chatting with friends or only God knew what. Normally, Ben would remind them that phones weren't allowed at the table, but he was too distracted this morning. He wasn't old, at least not in his own mind, but he couldn't fathom how people could stare at those tiny screens constantly day in and day out. He usually forgot his own cell phone at the office.

There were a thousand things for Ben to worry about when it came to his kids and their connections to the out-side world these days. Not just sexting—what an awful word that was—but also the way anyone could pretend to be any-thing on the Internet. There were predators lurking in the great big world out there and they didn't even need to hide in the dark anymore. He trusted his kids, and he thought he and Jennifer had raised them right, but you never quite knew what might be going through the head of a teenager. They could get themselves into a heap of trouble over the stupidest of decisions, especially a fleeting idea that seemed like a good one at the time.

To make matters worse for Ben, he was being forced to accept that his little girl wasn't so little anymore, no mat-ter how much he protested she was growing up way too fast. Mary was a freshman and she already had the boys swarming around her like swamp mosquitos.

Ben was still bothered by the memory of the two teen-age boys who had been staring and practically following them from aisle to aisle at the supermarket a few weeks ago. At first he had assumed it was because his uniform and the big Glock on his hip had caught their attention. He felt like kicking him-self when he finally realized they were watching and following and gawking at Mary. He resisted the urge to walk over there and show those boys the Glock close-up, just to make sure they knew she was off limits. Doing something like that wouldn't exactly be leading the community by example, now would it? Still... he'd be a liar if he didn't admit he was tempted.

Ben had dealt with Paul coming of age a lot easier, probably because sons would always be different than daughters in their father's eyes and mind and heart. Paul was now a high school senior, taller than his father by nearly three inches, and in two weeks he would step up on the stage of the school's auditorium and give his valedictorian speech to his fellow classmates and half the community. He had served as captain of the football squad, leading them to the state finals and a 12-2 record, in addition to earning All-State honors two years in a row. An academic scholarship to Penn State, where Paul would study either pre-law or political science, was waiting.

Ben looked forward to spending as much of the summer as possible with Paul hunting and fishing, just the two of them. Family time was great, but father-son time was special. It always had been with the two of them.

"Kids, no phones at the table," Jennifer said, delivering the usual tray of eggs, bacon, and toast.

She gave Ben a look but didn't say more. The distraction on his face was obvious. They had been high school sweethearts and she knew him better than anyone in the world. They had clicked immediately and they had planned on marriage before they even went to their first prom. For their first date, Ben had taken Jennifer to the State Police firing range where he had gained access privileges by winning the Bench Rest category at the Western PA Shooting Competition as a freshman. Most of her friends had thought that was such a redneck idea of a date, but she had absolutely loved it. What she loved even more was when she beat Ben the next year at that same shooting competition. They had finished first and second. True love, sometimes thy name is a properly sighted Remington 700 ADL scoped rifle.

"Why do we even have to go to school this week?" Mary asked, sliding her phone into her pocket and then scooping scrambled eggs onto her plate.

"We could at least take Friday off, right?" Paul suggested. He might be this year's valedictorian, but he was still a teenager at heart.

"Well, if you two are really good, you can help your dad and me clean out the garage this weekend. Spring cleaning keeps getting pushed off this year for some reason."

Both kids groaned, but the reaction was good-natured. Spring cleaning meant the kayaks and other summer gear would be pulled from the storage attic above the garage, and that could only be considered a good thing. Summer vacation was almost really here, and they both had big plans for their endless days of freedom.

"Speaking of summer," Mary said, "Emily, Madison, and Hailey are planning a trip in June to Hershey Park. Emily's mom will be driving and we'll be staying overnight at the Hershey Hotel."

"*We?*" Jennifer asked.

"Well, you know, if you and Dad say it's okay."

"I'll get back to you on that," Jennifer replied, preparing her own plate. She didn't have time to waste, she was showing a client a hunting cabin at nine. Being the only full-time real estate agent in Windbrook had its perks, such as very little competition, but it also meant she never had a day off. Not a lot of houses changed hands in the town proper, but tons of cabins and wooded building sites sold in the surrounding areas.

The phone rang and Ben hurried to answer it. The only person who called the house this early was the deputy on duty if something came up. Clients called Jennifer's cell phone, and Ben couldn't remember the last time the kids used the landline.

"Sheriff Logan," he answered. He stood and listened. "Holy hell. Okay, secure the scene. I'm on my way."

Ben hung up the phone and then stood there for a moment as if lost in thought.

"What happened?" Jennifer finally asked.

Ben turned to his wife and said, "Someone ran over Earl Duberstein's widow."

"Someone ran over Betty?" Jennifer asked, as if she didn't understand what the phrase meant. She stared at Ben, confused, ready for him to say it was some weird joke even though he and his men would never joke about something as awful as this.

Ben simply nodded. "Yes, right outside her house. Hit and run."

"Is she okay?"

Ben glanced at the kids, then back to his wife again. He shook his head—no, she's a long way from being okay—and kissed Jennifer good-bye as he passed the table and started for the front door. He had no idea this particular breakfast would be the family's last happy moments together. If so, he might have refused to leave and instead spent more time with his wife and kids. Betty Duberstein wasn't getting any deader, after all.

But, like most of us on the morning of the worst day of our life, he didn't know. He never even gave the idea a moment's consideration as he hurried out the door.

7.

PETER MYERS, THE DEPUTY ON duty for the graveyard shift, had already done a nice job of contaminating the crime scene by vomiting next to Betty Duberstein's body, but Sheriff Logan could hardly blame him. They had all seen death in this town, but most of those deaths came in the form of heart attacks and natural causes and hunting accidents. Lots of hunting accidents.

Deputy Myers had never lived outside of Windbrook, certainly hadn't seen the things Sheriff Logan saw in the war, and he didn't even watch scary movies, so his reaction to the grisly sight in front of the Duberstein home wasn't unusual.

This isn't right, Sheriff Logan thought, studying the body, *this isn't something that happens here.*

But it *had* happened here, and there was work to do, so he composed himself and cleared his throat.

"Who found her?" he asked, draping the sheet back over what remained of her head. Someone had probably thought they were helping by bringing that sheet out from their linen closet, but all they had done was further contaminate the scene. It couldn't be helped now.

"Joe Thompson, while delivering the morning paper," Deputy Myers said, choking back another wave of nausea.

"Where is he?" Sheriff Logan asked, looking around for Joe's battered station wagon. There were dozens of neighbors standing behind the yellow crime scene tape Deputy Myers had looped from the white picket fence at the edge of the Duberstein property to the trees on the other side of the street, creating a rectangle that every civilian recognized from television and respected out of custom.

"He called it in and then kept delivering the morning paper."

"He did *what?*"

"He kept..."

"Paul, I heard you, I just can't believe it."

"Do you think he had anything to do with this?"

"Jesus, I don't know. Joe's a drunk but he's always been harmless unless you count pinching the butts of the servers at Anderson's Bar. Go find him, right now, okay?"

"Yes, sir," Deputy Myers said, giving a salute. The expression on his face betrayed the unspoken thoughts in his head: he was grateful to be getting away from the corpse.

"Jesus Christ," Sheriff Logan muttered as he crouched next to the body again.

This just wasn't right. He closed his eyes and the memory of the nightmare flashed in the darkness: his town in ruin and those piles of skulls. He opened his eyes again and stared at the sheet, which had originally been white but was now wet and spreading scarlet.

He didn't need to examine the body again to understand what had happened here. Betty Duberstein had been starting or finishing her morning walk when someone jumped the curb and slammed on the brakes just as they struck her, sending her flying. Judging from the black skid marks that stretched from the road to the sidewalk, he estimated the driver had probably been doing forty or fifty miles per hour, an unheard of speed in this neighborhood with its narrow streets.

The impact probably wouldn't have been survivable, especially not at Betty's age when every bone seems to be made of porcelain, just waiting for the slightest provocation to break, but the driver had made sure to finish the job.

There were burnout marks from the driver accelerating, gaining speed again before he or she ran over Betty's head, flattening it in an instant, sending her eyeballs bursting from their sockets and her brains exploding out of her ears. Her hair was a bloody mess and broken teeth littered the ground around her crushed mouth. Bloody tire tracks led away from the body, back onto the street toward the middle of town. There was so much blood, more than a human body seemed capable of containing.

Could the driver have run Betty over the second time in a panic as he or she fled the scene? Unlikely, considering two of his tires would have been on the sidewalk and the other two would have been on the street, meaning he had to fight to keep the wheel straight and lined up with his target. It had to be intentional.

"Aw, shit," Sheriff Logan whispered.

8.

DEPUTY MYERS PULLED INTO THE gravel driveway leading to Joe Thompson's shack and managed to open the patrol car's door just in time to vomit onto the lawn instead of all over his steering wheel. It wasn't just the image of Betty Duberstein's squashed head that kept tripping his stomach, it was also the appalling smells still clinging to the inside of his nose. His throat burned from the flood of acid washing up and out of his mouth. His breakfast was long gone.

"My Lord," he muttered, closing the door again and wiping his sleeve across his face.

He started the patrol car rolling down the gravel driveway toward the dilapidated shack with a rusted metal roof and plywood where the windows once were. Trees towered over the home, such as it was, and the property was littered with the dead leaves of the previous fall. Parked sideways by the front door was Joe Thompson's station wagon, which Deputy Meyer would recognize anywhere. He was shocked it passed inspection each year and he suspected Joe's habit of drinking late into the early hours of the morning with more than a few of the mechanics at Pepper's Garage had something to do with that.

"Base, this is Unit Four at Joe Thompson's house. His car is here, and I'm proceeding to question him about this morning's incident, over," Deputy Meyer said into the radio.

"Roger that," replied Deputy Dayton, who was manning the office alone this morning. "Watch your ass, okay? Over."

Deputy Meyer planned on doing exactly that. He got out of the car and listened closely for anything that might indicate where Joe was. Meyer had been on this job for nearly five years, had never drawn his weapon in the line of duty, but he popped that cherry without thought. With his Glock in hand, he approached the crooked wooden door of the shack.

"Joe Thompson, this is Deputy Meyer. We need to talk."

No reply from inside.

Deputy Meyer stood to the side of the door, double-checking his surroundings for any sign of movement or life. There was nothing. All was quiet.

Staying out of the line of possible fire as he had been trained, he knocked heavily on the door, which was so flimsy it shuddered under his fist.

"Listen, Joe, this will be easier if you let me know where you are. I wouldn't want there to be any kind of... misunderstanding, you know what I mean?"

Still no reply.

Silence wasn't good. Like most of the citizens in Windbrook, Joe Thompson owned at least one hunting rifle, maybe more.

If Joe had killed Betty and was now lying in wait to take out the first person who came for him, or even to set-up a suicide by cop scenario, Deputy Meyer really didn't want to kick open the door and be all alone for whatever followed.

He was about to back slowly to his car to radio for assistance when he heard a noise from inside the shack. At first he thought the sound might be a hungry cat crying, but then the cries turned to gurgles like someone fighting to breathe. Deputy Meyer's first instinct was that something had happened to Joe and the man needed help. His second instinct was that Joe had someone in there and something bad was happening to that person. Either way, there was no time to waste.

"Joe, I'm coming in, get your hands where I can see them!" Deputy Meyer called. He took a deep breath and put his shoulder into the door, which exploded off the rusty hinges as if it had been hanging by a thread to begin with.

The inside of the shack was bathed in darkness and stank like a chicken roost. Meyer tried the light switch by the door, but there was no power. He flipped his Maglite on, raised it next to his Glock, and swept the room.

At first, he couldn't see anything clearly through the piles of old, moldy newspapers. There had to be hundreds of stacks, some as tall as the ceiling, all of them leaning this way or that way as if they might collapse in the slightest of breeze.

"Jesus H. Hoarder," Deputy Meyer whispered, sweeping the room again.

The circle of light crossed something in the narrow path between the mountains of old news and Meyer snapped the flashlight back to that spot. There was a bloody shoe print on the dirty floor, still fresh based on the way the blood reflected the light.

"Joe Thompson, this is Deputy Meyer, do you hear me? I need to know where you are and I need to see your hands right now!"

Another muffled gurgle, and this time Meyer honed in on the location of the sound. The room beyond this trash pile, most likely the kitchen. He made his way through the canyon of newspaper piles, carefully avoiding the bloody shoe print.

When his light crisscrossed the kitchen, he couldn't believe what he saw, but he was instantly grateful his stomach was empty because the dry heaves started again.

Joe Thompson was strung up in the middle of the room, one arm tied to the top of the cabinets on the left and the other arm tied to the top of the cabinets on the right. His hands dangled loosely, obviously broken at the wrist, and blood dripped from the fingertips. He was naked and his crotch was a gory mess of flayed flesh, ripped hair, and open wounds. His toes had been removed with something like an electric turkey knife. They were hanging on a thread around his neck.

"He was not a very nice man," a voice said softly behind Deputy Meyer.

Meyer spun in a panic, his finger depressing the trigger of his Glock and sending two rounds into the floor as his weapon rose to find a target.

"Woah, woah, woah there son," the owner of the voice said, his wooden and silver cane whipping around from his side and stopping the rising firearm in one smooth move.

"Who are you?" Deputy Meyer asked, his heart pounding and his eyes flicking back and forth from the old man's face to the cane that was stopping his service weapon at a 45-degree angle to his side. It was as if the cane had somehow paralyzed

his arm. He couldn't move the gun or pull the trigger again if his life depended on it.

"I am but a foolish old man," the stranger said, "and I came to this town looking for a few good souls to make me believe in humanity again."

"I don't understand."

"That's okay, Peter Meyer, that's not important. What *is* important is you and I need to have a talk about dreams and hopes and plans for the future. Joe Thompson there had a dream about bringing a little boy here, just snatching him off the street, did you know that?"

Deputy Meyer shook his head. Joe was known as a drunk who sometimes got a little mean when deep in his cups, but he was supposed to be mostly harmless.

"Your Joe Thompson was most definitely not harmless," the old man said as if he had read the deputy's mind. "And there are even more dangerous people in this town of yours."

"There are?" Deputy Meyer asked, no longer thinking about the gun frozen at the end of his hand but instead watching the way the old man's eyes seemed to be changing color. He could have sworn they were gray at first, but the lack of light in here made seeing things difficult, and now they were more of a green.

"Oh yes, most certainly. First, though, before we continue, you need to tell me about your secret dream."

"My secret dream...?"

"That's right, Deputy. Everyone has one."

And so Deputy Meyer spoke, like so many people before him had; people who had been found lacking and judged accordingly once they had served their purpose for the old man.

9.

SHERIFF LOGAN PULLED HIS CAR into a vacant parking spot in front of the Windbrook Diner, remnants of last night's dream flitting through his mind like a tumbleweed in a windstorm. All of his deputies were out searching for Joe Thompson now that the State Police had arrived and secured the crime scene. Ben needed a few minutes to sit and think, but he didn't want to return to the office yet. He couldn't shake the feeling that more was wrong in his town than just the first hit-and-run murder in nearly forty years.

Bill Smith was working the grill and singing along to an old Rolling Stones tune, and he saw Ben and waved and flipped a burger, all in the same smooth motion. Bill was born in Windbrook and would die there, like most of the older residents. At seventy-seven, he would never beat his personal best running the mile again, but he still managed to mind the store every day. Bill was a solid citizen, but more importantly to Ben, he was a friend.

"Hey old man, how's life treating you?" Ben asked as the heavy glass door that had greeted Bill's customers since he was a kid slid closed behind him.

"Ah, not too bad, Sheriff, and stop calling me old man before I hop over this counter and teach you some manners," Bill said, smiling. He still possessed the same mischievous, childlike twinkle in his eyes that had been present when he had snuck free ice cream to a shy four-year-old Ben.

"What's the news about Betty Duberstein?" Bill asked, his face turning serious.

Normally, Ben wouldn't share information about an ongoing investigation with a civilian, but this was Bill and there was no one else in the restaurant to overhear the conversation. Ben knew the town was already abuzz with the news and the rumor mill would be running wild, but Bill was someone he could trust and count on. He always had been.

"Still no clue what happened. Joe Thompson's the only witness and we can't find him anywhere."

"Joe couldn't have done it," Bill said. "He chases skirts and drinks too much, but he'd never hurt no one."

"Yeah, that's my take, too, but if it wasn't Joe, that means we have no leads until the State Police come back with more info about the tire treads. They're narrowing down the make and model as we speak."

Bill stared at the sheriff for a moment, eyeing him up and down as if he had never seen him before.

"You don't seem yourself, Ben. I heard Betty was pretty messed up. That dragging you down?"

"I don't know," Ben said, being more honest with Bill than he would have been with anyone else other than Jennifer. "I had a nightmare last night, a bad one, and I just can't shake it. Then this shitty mess with Betty Duberstein happens. Something feels off in town today, but I can't put my finger on what."

Bill studied the sheriff for another moment. "You know, next time I see Jennifer I'm gonna tell her to take you on a vacation. I think you need one."

Ben's lips parted in a slight smile. "Yeah, you might be right. We'll see how the rest of the day goes."

"Sheriff, you there? Over," came the muffled voice from the radio on Ben's hip.

"I'm here, what do you have, over?"

"You're not going to believe this. You need to meet us at Snyder's Garage ASAP. Over."

"Snyder's Garage? That dump's been closed for years. Over."

"Roger that, but I don't want to say more over this party line. It's pretty awful. Over."

10.

JASON SINCLAIR'S DELIVERY TRUCK WAS parked behind Snyder's Garage, which looked every day of the ten long years it had been abandoned. The pavement was cracked and broken, bushes at the edge of the property had grown huge and ungainly with no one to trim them back each season, and every window had been broken by bored teenagers throwing rocks.

Sheriff Logan pulled around to where Deputy Jones and Deputy Wilson were carefully encircling another crime scene with yellow police tape. Both of them were pasty white going on green.

"Where's Deputy Meyer?" Logan asked after getting out of his cruiser.

"Not sure, boss," Wilson replied. "Deputy Dayton is manning the station alone, but he's been putting out the call to Meyer for thirty minutes now with no reply. Thinks maybe the cruiser's radio went bad."

I wouldn't bet on that, the sheriff thought, the uneasy feeling in his gut kicking into overdrive. "What have we got here?"

"A real shit show, that's what we got. Something is ten shades of fucked up around here this morning, boss."

"Watch the language, Steve."

"Sorry, boss, but go see for yourself."

Sheriff Logan walked to the open door of the delivery truck, taking care to avoid any shoe prints or other possible evidence. He peered inside and immediately understood what his deputy had meant.

He didn't know Jason Sinclair well since the deliveryman lived in Glenton and normally never came further into town than Joe Thompson's place, but he recognized the delivery truck and the dead man inside it.

Only dead didn't accurately describe what had been done to him.

Jason Sinclair was slumped in the driver's seat, his wide eyes staring blankly out the windshield. His eyelids had been removed, three of the fingers on his right hand were missing, and one of them was sticking out from between his teeth like the stub of a cigar. His shirt was stained maroon with his blood and a symbol had been drawn there in ragged lines: a peace sign.

"Somebody find me Peter Meyer ASAP," Sheriff Logan said, making his way back outside the yellow police tape. "He was headed to Joe Thompson's shack, right?"

"Yes, sir," Deputy Wilson replied.

"Okay, Wilson, you go and don't you waste a second. Radio me the minute you get there."

"You think Joe did this, too?" Wilson asked.

"I have no idea, but we have a man out of radio contact and we need to find him, fast."

"What should I do, boss?" Deputy Jones asked.

"Secure the scene, radio the staties for support, and don't let anyone else behind this garage. No one sees inside that truck who isn't a LEO, you understand?"

"Yes, sir."

Sheriff Logan returned to his cruiser, backed up, and peeled out onto Snyder Avenue, which was named after the long dead family who had built the garage and run it for over forty years.

"Shit show," Logan muttered as he drove away. "That's an understatement. What the hell is going on today?"

11.

THE OLD MAN WAS STANDING at the corner of Main Street and Prince Avenue, watching the door to Windbrook Realty and Titles, Jennifer Logan's home away from home. She was at her desk writing an offer on a hunting cabin she had showed that morning, and the old man could see her through the enormous front window with the business name stenciled across it.

"Such a hard worker, Mrs. Logan," the old man said. "I wonder if you'd like for your husband's nightmares to disappear. I wonder what you'd be willing to trade for that to happen."

The old man watched her work and he smiled as he contemplated what her secret wish might be and what she might be willing to do to make it happen. Off in the distance, a bell started ringing at the community school. Soon the children of Windbrook would be free to run and play and forget their educational troubles. Ah, to be young again.

The old man's smile grew into a toothy grin. It was such a beautiful day and he couldn't wait to offer his special deal to a few more people. Maybe someone would surprise him today after all.

You just never knew. Not on a beautiful day like this. Almost anything could happen.

12.

SHERIFF LOGAN SLAMMED ON THE brakes as he passed by the Windbrook Diner on Main Street. Something wasn't right. The CLOSED sign hung in the front window and there was a red stain splashed across the window glass.

He parked and hurried to the door, which was locked, something it had never been during business hours in his entire life as far as he knew.

"Bill?" Sheriff Logan called. "You in there?"

He studied the stain and he didn't have to think twice before smashing the glass door with his heavy Maglite. He had seen more than enough blood in his lifetime to recognize it drying on a window.

13.

"HELLO THERE," THE OLD MAN said. "Could I ask you a question?"

His demeanor was friendly, his suit was neatly pressed, and his black fedora hat made him look like your favorite grandfather.

Of course, the answer came, *of course you can ask me your question.*

So he asked, and as always, he was told the deep, dark truth of the person's most guarded secret desire.

He was always told. Always.

People found his strange eyes to be irresistible.

14.

SHERIFF LOGAN STEPPED OVER THE broken glass and he discovered what he most feared.

Bill Smith was dead, slumped in a booth by the window, the side of his head splattered onto the glass. Clots of blood and hair and dark shiny brain tissue glistened on the tabletop.

Splayed against the counter where Ben had drunk a thousand milkshakes as a kid was Deputy Meyer, his service weapon dangling in his limp hand. After executing Bill, he had shot himself in both legs and bled out all over the black and white checkered floor.

"Jesus, help us," Sheriff Logan whispered. He felt like he was losing his mind. None of this made any sense. None of it.

He turned his back on the scene, struggling to maintain his composure. These men were his friends. Good, steadfast men. It didn't make any damn sense.

He was out of deputies in the field to call upon, so he radioed the State Police barracks and explained what was happening.

"Additional officers are on the way," the young man on the other end said in an excited voice.

"Send everyone you can," the sheriff replied. Then he returned to his car and took the necessary steps to secure the scene.

In the back of his head, a little voice suggested he call Jennifer and tell her to go straight home and lock the doors and windows and not let anyone in, but that voice was drowned out by a thousand other louder voices delving into what Ben had seen and done so far today, trying to connect the dots and make sense of the senseless.

Thoughts of Jennifer melted away into the chaos, and he didn't think of her again until it was much too late.

15.

ACROSS TOWN, THE FINAL BELL of the day was ringing at the Community School, and Jennifer Logan was on her way to pick up her kids for the last time.

16.

FORTY MINUTES LATER, THE STATE Police had arrived at the Windbrook Diner and Sheriff Logan was back in his car. Now Deputy Dayton wasn't answering the radio in the station.

Sheriff Logan drove along Main Street in the middle of town, his eyes scanning for anything out of place, but *everything* felt wrong and out of place given how the day had gone. CLOSED signs hung in several storefronts and the sidewalks seemed much emptier than usual for this time of day, but the sheriff didn't stop to investigate. He was in too much of a hurry to check the station and reestablish communication with his men.

The sheriff glanced at the darkening sky as he drove out of the town proper. Even the weather had changed for the worse out of nowhere. Clusters of black thunderclouds spotted the slate gray sky, screening the sun's rays. A strengthening wind swept down from the east carrying the promise of rain.

Sheriff Logan carefully steered around a wide bend in the road and that was when he saw the parking lot for the

Windbrook Grocery and Farmer's Market. People were running and cutting across the lot with their heads down, scurrying behind cars like children playing a game of tag or hide-and-seek.

These weren't kids playing games, though. They were people of all ages, fleeing in fear, trying to hide, screaming and running, running for their lives.

And then Sheriff Logan heard the gunshots.

17.

GUNFIRE ECHOED ACROSS THE VALLEY, and this time it wasn't coming from hunters in the state parks.

Sheriff Logan hit his siren and swung into the parking lot where the dead and wounded were scattered across the pavement. A few crumpled bodies lay perfectly still, others hugged the gravel lot in terror, and one man was trying to drag himself to safety, leaving a bloody smear behind him.

The shooter was nowhere to be seen as far as Sheriff Logan could tell, but he pulled the patrol car as close as he could to the crawling man to block him from further fire. Glock in hand, the sheriff got out, knelt behind the car door, and called to the man. He had stopped crawling and rolled onto his side. The sheriff, staring at the gaping hole in the man's stomach, could see why. The man had been hold-ing a clump of his intestines when he died. His stomach organs were squirming in between and around his curled fingers like worms, his digestive juices spilling onto the lot. The man's face was frozen in death, his mouth hooked in a death-fighting snarl. The dead man, Logan realized to his horror, was Windbrook's former sheriff, Leroy Callahaun.

Fighting the panic rising in his own stomach, Sheriff Logan sprinted behind a green Buick with a shattered windshield. Chips of asphalt stung his arms and legs as bullets tore into the parking lot. The shooter was still active, but where the hell was he? People were crying out in pain and panic and yelling at the sheriff from all directions, but he only caught snatches of words and sentences. "I'm hit... started shooting... my arm... Christ Almighty... think she's dead... help us... please... where is he... Lord Jesus, please help... help..."

At first, the sheriff thought one of the shoppers had gone berserk or that maybe there was a robbery-gone-wrong in progress, but now he realized the gunfire was coming from a higher elevation, from the tree-covered hillside behind the store. A sniper who knew how to pick a strong vantage point.

Sheriff Logan gazed through the windows of the green Buick, scanning the series of steep cliffs that marked the edge of town. After a long breathless moment, he spotted a fire flash in the trees as another shot rang out. *Bingo.*

The sheriff scooted to the back of the Buick and peeked around the trunk, searching the parking lot for any wounded in the line of fire. He was relieved to see that they all had reached safety with the others. He didn't want to go out there again if he didn't have—

Logan's heart skipped a beat and then almost stopped when he glanced to his far right and saw it:

Jennifer's car was parked neatly in a space not far from the store's entrance. He scanned the parking lot again, but he didn't see Jennifer or the kids anywhere. His heart jerked in his chest and his lungs felt deflated and heavy.

"Jennifer!" he yelled as loud as he could muster. "Paul! Mary!"

He was answered by another gunshot, the sound of breaking glass, and the muffled sobs of a scared teenaged girl hiding nearby. *Whoever was up on that hill was a hell of a shot.*

"Jennifer!" he called again, louder this time.

There was no answer.

Where the hell were they?

Dying?

Dead?

A mental image of Jennifer squirming on the ground, her hands grasping her bullet-riddled stomach, flashed in Sheriff Logan's mind and he squeezed his eyes shut, pushing it away.

18.

SHERIFF LOGAN SWALLOWED HIS FEAR and panic. It was his sworn duty to protect this town and he intended to do just that. He quickly informed nearby civilians of the shooter's location and yelled at them to remain where they were until more help arrived. He desperately needed to call for backup, but he had left his radio in the car, which was too far away to reach safely, and his cell phone was sitting forgotten on his desk back at the office again. He always forgot that damn thing when he needed it the most.

I should have called in before I left the car, he scolded himself. Someone inside the store must have called 911, though, by now. But it was his job, not theirs.

Sheriff Logan knew he had to do something and do something quick. He couldn't just wait here and let the shooter flank them. If that happened, they'd all be sitting ducks, like targets in a shooting gallery. He spotted a pair of green dumpsters at the far end of the parking lot. The seconds ticked on his watch as he breathed deeply, steadying himself. He wondered again: *who the hell is on that hill?*

The thought barely had time to register in his mind when he bolted from safety.

19.

SHERIFF LOGAN WEAVED ACROSS THE parking lot bracing for the burning lead impact of a bullet. His ears strained for the quick burst of gunfire, but the shots never came. He slipped behind the dumpsters, sucking in huge gulps of air. Why hadn't the sniper fired a shot? Maybe he'd already fled. Or maybe he was moving into a better position to pick off more victims.

Other questions surfaced as Sheriff Logan contemplated his next move.

Where was his backup? Someone had to have called for help by now. The State Police could be here in a matter of minutes if they were coming from the diner. Maybe less.

Leroy Callahaun was dead. The man who had hired him and given him a new purpose in life was now a corpse growing cold on the pavement of the Windbrook Grocery and Farmer's Market.

How many more were dead or wounded?

His own family?

Please, God, no.

Sheriff Logan checked his watch and realized only ten minutes had passed since he'd left the diner. That meant he had been at the scene for only four or five minutes at the most.

He carefully leaned his head around the dumpster. The wood's edge was maybe fifteen yards away, beckoning him. Staring at the broken row of trees, he knew what he had to do.

He lifted his Glock in front of him, moved to the side of the dumpster, and then broke into a dead sprint for the tree line. As the trees grew closer, he left his feet, diving for cover among the green shrubs. He hit the ground hard and rolled to his knees behind a tangle of thick brush. His left hand was bleeding from where he had landed on a piece of shattered bottle, but he ignored the blood, realizing again that he had drawn no fire. Maybe the sniper had really left.

The sheriff edged his way around a fallen, decaying tree and crawled on his belly to the next natural barrier. The process of moving from cover position to cover position was intimately familiar to him. How many times had he participated in this exercise in his teens and early twenties? Without sparing the thought, he flashed back to boot camp. *Life was but a wheel, spinning 'round and 'round again, everything old was new again.*

He made his way slowly and carefully up the steep hill, hurrying to stay behind the protection of the old growth trees, stopping every few minutes to listen for movement ahead. A novice might believe he was alone in these woods, but Ben Logan wasn't a mere beginner at the world's most dangerous version of hide-and-seek.

A long peal of thunder sounded above the trees, startling him. The storm rolling into the valley was quickly turning day into night, and the shadows jumped and chased after him.

Feeling very much like the soldier of his youth, Sheriff Logan became one with those shadows.

20.

THE SHERIFF PAUSED BELOW AN outcropping of enormous rocks, wiping both hands on his pants, removing the greasy sweat. When he was finished, he regripped his Glock and continued stealthily forward. His shirt was soaked and his face and arms were scraped raw and bleeding from the dozens of thorn bushes blocking his progress. He squinted into the murky woods ahead, studying the trees and the darker spaces in between. The woods were still and silent around him. Even the animals had gone quiet. Each time he halted his progress he heard only his own thundering heartbeat.

After what seemed like endless climbing, he stumbled across what he was looking for. Scattered at his feet were several dozen empty cartridges. A small army of red ants swarmed among the tiny shells.

Gazing down the hill, the sheriff was awed by the sight before him. From this over-watch position, the sniper had a perfect view of the parking lot. The nearby buildings were laid out like a miniature scale model in some architect's office.

But the distance was incredible. Just as Ben wasn't a novice to making war, neither was the shooter. To actually hit and kill moving targets from here was the work of a professional shooter, maybe one of the best he had ever seen.

The sheriff spotted his cruiser among the other cars, and the tiny still bodies of those people he hadn't been able to help. None of his deputies or the staties were in sight.

Where the hell is my backup? he thought. They should have been there by now. Something else must have gone very wrong in town for no one to respond to an active shooter situation.

Logan visually retraced his path from the cruiser to the edge of the woods and felt even more confused. The sniper had a bird's eye view of everything, and his path had been out in the open for at least thirty-five yards.

This guy could have easily blown me away, he thought. *So why did he decide to cut and run?*

Before the sheriff could consider the question any further, something moved behind him.

21.

THE SHERIFF REGISTERED THE MOVEMENT and reacted before his brain even processed the source of the sound, his old military training kicking into high gear. He dropped to his stomach at the sound of dry, crackling branches under approaching feet and slid himself under a thick bush.

Why was the shooter coming back now? He wasn't finished? Maybe went for more ammo? But that wouldn't have been very professional, not to have been carrying enough on him for whatever grisly task he meant to accomplish.

The sheriff further concealed himself with overgrown ferns, his hand squeezing into his gun's grooved handgrip. The footsteps crunched louder as they drew nearer and with each step the sheriff's heart gained momentum.

The approaching figure was making too much noise for the sheriff's liking. The person who had made those amazingly brutal shots had to be a professional soldier and a pro wouldn't be moving so loudly. He would be quiet and precise in his steps.

Sheriff Logan glanced upward through a gap in the trees. The bloated storm clouds had gained strength in the battle for the sky and the forest grew darker in what seemed like a matter of seconds. A blanket of darkness was drifting down upon him, smothering him in night during the middle of day.

Straining through the gloomy grayness, the sheriff watched as a ghost-like figure emerged from the shadows, cutting through the waist-high shrubbery—and walked directly toward him.

22.

A BRIGHT FLASH OF LIGHTNING illuminated the sky, sending jagged shadows across the small clearing where the sniper had set up position to target the parking lot.

Sheriff Logan could barely make out the faint outline of the person in the flickering darkness. It had to be the shooter. Tall and thin and carrying a rifle, stopping twenty yards short of Logan's position. The sheriff couldn't quite see what the shooter was doing but reloading the rifle seemed likely from the controlled movements. The idea of opening fire on the unsuspecting shooter crossed the sheriff's mind but he quickly decided against it. If he shot him in the back, the sheriff would be no better than the murdering bastard.

Sheriff Logan quietly shifted his weight, clinching his jaw tight, holding his breath. His fingers tightened on his weapon. *Should he rush the shooter? Could he cover that much ground in time? What if—*

Another bolt of lightning scratched the black sky, and the sniper turned, revealing his identity.

23.

SHOCK TWISTED THE SHERIFF'S FACE into a mask of agony as he recognized the person standing before him. He felt a sledgehammer sucker punch land in his stomach and he had to steady himself on his elbow to remain still.

A spectacular series of white flashes stabbed at the sky, giving the sheriff another, better view of the sniper.

He saw his son's smiling face.

24.

BEN LOGAN'S HEART STOPPED DEAD. Air refused to enter his lungs. A tornado of emotions shook his body with uncontrollable pain and confusion. It felt like he was stuck in one of his nightmares and couldn't wake up yet nothing had ever been more real than this moment before him. His son was a killer. But how? Why? The idea didn't make any sense.

Paul laid a dark red scarf on the ground and spread more shells on it. The sheriff immediately recognized the scarf; it was his wife's favorite, a Christmas present from two winters ago. Crouched on one knee, Paul loaded the rifle, whistling happily as if he were merely at the firing range for a fun afternoon of target practice.

Sheriff Logan edged out from under the bush, scraping his back on a heavy dead branch.

Paul continued to sort the shells, unaware that he wasn't alone.

The sheriff stood, bending sore muscles and started toward his son. He walked slowly, still unsure of what he would do. His eyes were filled with tears and his Glock hung loosely from his right hand; his finger was not on the trigger.

The sheriff was ten yards short of his son's position when Paul spun suddenly and pointed the rifle at his head—and smiled.

25.

"HI, DAD."

The sheriff jerked to a stop, opened his mouth to speak, but no words came out.

"C'mon, Dad, you taught me better than to let myself be snuck up on in the woods."

"What... what the hell are you doing, Paul?"

His son's expression remained unchanged. His mouth was smiling, but his eyes were cold and dark. The eyes of a stranger.

The air reeked of death and hung heavy like smog around the boy. Ben could taste it on his lips. He saw a wildness, a hint of something not entirely human, in Paul's eyes, and for a moment he thought he might turn and run away from his son.

"Explain to me. Please. What are you doing here?"

Paul looked directly into his father's confused eyes and laughed.

The sound was evil.

26.

"I THINK YOU KNOW EXACTLY what he's doing here," a voice said from behind the sheriff.

Ben turned and watched the old man in the black suit reveal himself from behind a tree.

"You?" Sheriff Logan said.

"Do you *know* me?" the old man asked, genuinely surprised.

The sheriff nodded. "I've seen you before. In a dream. You were standing on Main Street, surrounded by fire and death and skulls."

"Yes, that does sound like me," the old man mused. "I've been waiting to meet you all day. I've already met your deputies and some of the other fine people of your town. Well, maybe not so fine of people. I had such hopes for them."

"How have you done this? *Why* have you done this?"

"It's what I do, Benjamin. It's my duty, you could say."

"What did you do to Paul?"

"Well, he told me he would do anything to see his deepest, most secret dream come true. I told him I could help him with that, but I needed a small favor in return."

"Favor?"

"That's right. He had to shoot your wife and daughter and a few other people. He's a very good shot, you know? Must be in his genes. But here's the rub. He still had a choice to make. He could say no and walk away. Do you understand that? He had to choose to move forward with our agreement. I'm many things, but I'm not a sneak."

"You're insane, aren't you?"

"Me? You're the one who dreamed of me, remember? You dreamed of me and invited me here."

"I never invited you here!"

"Benjamin, I only come to the willing. Time and space mean nothing to me. I simply go where I'm wanted." He paused. "Where I'm needed. You called me here whether you realize it or not. Joe Thompson, Jason Sinclair, Peter Meyer, and now Paul welcomed me into their hearts and minds. They all asked for my help, so I gave them a choice, and they got something in return." The old man snapped his long fingers. "Fair trade."

"I've seen what those first three got in return," Sheriff Logan said gravely.

"Well, in that case, perhaps I could do you a favor in exchange for you doing me one? I already know what your biggest desire is right now. You want your family back, correct?"

Sheriff Logan glanced at his son, who stared blankly at him with the rifle in his hands.

"Paul's already done what you wanted, hasn't he? He lured me here. Even if I do whatever you ask me to do, he's going to be repaid for what he's done, right? Like you repaid the others?"

The old man bit his upper lip to stop his grin from growing larger. "That *is* the way these deals often work."

"Okay," Sheriff Logan said, firing so quickly even he wasn't aware of his hand moving. He squeezed the trigger six times, hitting center mass all six times.

The old man simply stared at the sheriff, the six holes in his suit flapping in the breeze.

"How'd that work out for you?" the old man asked, smiling like a lunatic now, his mouth crammed with more sharp teeth than Ben thought humanly possible.

The old man didn't wait for an answer. He swung the cane at Sheriff Logan's head, but the lawman was already ducking to dodge the blow. The old man had done the same thing in the nightmare and Logan was not only expecting the quickness of the attack but he was also desperate to avoid the impact this time. He didn't want to experience whatever horrors the cane might bring.

But even though he moved as fast as he could, Ben didn't move fast enough.

The cane grazed the top of his head and a brilliant white light exploded all around him.

27.

AS THE WHITE LIGHT FLICKERED and then faded, Sheriff Logan found himself standing next to a smartly dressed twenty-something blonde woman with a microphone as if he were about to be interviewed by a reporter. Yet she didn't seem to notice him. She was facing a cameraman and behind the cameraman was the open door of a WTAE-TV ABC News van where a producer sat watching a handful of monitors. The van was parked as close to the Windbrook Grocery and Farmer's Market as the State Police would allow. It was night now and there were dozens of police officers and crime scene investigators spread across the scene. Another dozen news vans were parked along the street leading to the market.

From the reporter's earpiece, Sheriff Logan heard the story being thrown her way:

"And now for more on that horrifying story out of Windbrook, Pennsylvania, we go to Cynthia Haddonsmith for a live update."

"Tom," she said right on cue, "in a horrible twist of irony, Sheriff Benjamin Logan's 17-year-old son, Paul, was one of the first witnesses to reach the scene. As you can see in this footage uploaded by a local citizen, the young man slipped through police barricades and broke down emotionally at the sight of his deceased mother and 14-year-old sister. In yet another cruel twist of fate, only minutes later, he would learn about the heroic death of his father, Sheriff Benjamin Logan. Paul appeared to go into shock at the news and had to be helped from the area. Paul Logan is the graduating valedictorian at Windbrook Community School and the events of today have to be particularly heartbreaking for his classmates as they..."

While she spoke, Sheriff Logan walked between her and the camera and no one reacted. It was as if he were a ghost, but he suspected the truth was worse than that. He watched on the monitor as the shaky clip of Paul being restrained at a line of police tape played again and again.

"Police officials failed to reveal whether they have any leads on the case but they did clarify that they feel the sniper has left the immediate area."

The white light flashed again.

28.

TIME PASSED AND NOW SHERIFF Logan was standing in the rear of the Community School's auditorium. He wasn't surprised by who was standing on the stage before the capacity crowd, which included dozens of news cameras for the first time in Windbrook's history.

"And so," Paul Logan said, "I'd like to thank the faculty, my fellow students, and every member of this beautiful community, not only for your help throughout my high school career but for your generous and much-needed support and genuine caring over the last few weeks. I will be forever grateful. This is a joyous day in a sadly mournful time, but today will live in my memories forever, thanks to all of you. I know my mother and Mary are watching me right now and they are smiling down at all of us. I loved my father, your sheriff, neighbor and friend, as I know he loved all of you. And I know he would be proud of me on this afternoon, as I was of him, each and every day. Thank you."

The crowd rose to their feet, roaring their support and love for the boy-turned-man.

Paul waved and left the podium. He allowed a small grin to slip onto his face as he walked the length of the flower-lined stage and descended the decorated steps. He waved at an elegant, elderly gentleman dressed in a sparkling black suit. The man smiled and returned the wave.

The white light flashed again.

29.

WHEN THE BRIGHT LIGHT FADED, Sheriff Logan needed a moment to reorient himself. He stood next to two young women sitting on a bench in a park-like setting, but this wasn't any park he could ever remember visiting. Then he saw the resurrected statue of legendary football coach Joe Paterno and he understood where he was.

"What do you think is *really* happening?" the first girl said, pointing at the story that occupied the entire front page of the *Penn State Daily Collegian.*

"I don't know, but my parents are freaked. They want me to transfer to Slippery Rock to be closer to home."

"Slippery Cock, you mean," the first girl replied and giggled.

Sheriff Logan leaned over and skimmed the story that had generated the conversation.

Does Happy Valley Have A Serial Killer?
By Joseph Hill

Campus, local, and state police have been busy at Penn State during the last three months. Too busy.

In a scene that has become all too familiar at the

campus, police officers responded to another call last night concerning a missing college student.

Twenty-year-old political science major Tammy Stewart was reported missing by her roommate after she didn't return from a date the previous night. Police are questioning Ms. Stewart's roommates and classmates but have no clues as to the identity of her mystery date.

Over the last ten weeks, five male and female students have suddenly vanished without warning.

Police officials are warning all students to walk in groups after dusk and they will be enforcing the curfew...

30.

THE WHITE LIGHT FLASHED AGAIN, and this time Sheriff Logan knew exactly where he was, but it took him a moment to understand who was standing at the podium in front of the state capitol with the green dome looming behind him. Probably a dozen years had passed, and a media scrum surrounded the man, who looked too familiar for comfort for Logan.

"Thank you all for coming on such short notice. As you know, Doug Hemmings was my mentor in the District Attorney's office after I graduated from Penn State and we will not stop until his assassin has been brought to justice. But just as important is his legacy as a leader to our community, and it is with great reservation that I'm announcing I'll be continuing his campaign for Governor on behalf of the party."

Off to the side stood an elderly gentleman dressed in a sharp black suit, and Sheriff Logan was certain that man was Paul's true mentor, no matter what he said.

The light flashed again.

31.

THE BALLROOM WAS GRANDER THAN any Sheriff Logan had ever been in before, and standing on a dramatic stage before throngs of loyal supporters was an even older version of his son.

Balloons were drifting from the ceiling onto the stage and people were crying for joy and Paul was dancing with a beautiful woman in a red dress. His wife.

The enormous signs behind them declared, "Paul Logan For President! He Fixed Pennsylvania, He Can Fix Our Nation!"

Off to the side of the stage was the same elderly man who didn't appear to have aged a day since the events in Windbrook.

He grinned at Sheriff Logan.

32.

THE WHITE LIGHT FLASHED, AND this time the sheriff found himself in a dark conference room hundreds of feet below the Rocky Mountains.

A General whose uniform seemed to sag with medals was briefing President Logan.

"...in reaction to yesterday's nuclear strike against Beijing and surrounding areas, over one hundred Chinese missiles were launched, striking the east coast yesterday evening, leaving the capital and other eastern metropolitan areas, including New York, Philadelphia and Boston in complete destruction. The death toll is estimated in the millions."

"How safe are we here?" the President asked.

"Safe for now, sir," the General replied. "This base was purposely kept off all the books and all of the workers who built it last year were dealt with as you ordered."

"Excellent," Paul said, nodding at his most trusted adviser, the old man in the suit seated to his right. "What's our next move?"

33.

THE WHITE LIGHT FADED AWAY from Sheriff Logan's eyes, leaving his vision blurry with tears. He sat in the darkness under the trees, and he glanced from the old man to his son and back to the old man again.

His Glock was still gripped tightly in his hand, pointed at the old man's chest. The old man in the suit smiled.

"Choices are such a unique human problem, aren't they?" he asked. "Will you do as I ask of you, so you may be with your family again?"

Sheriff Logan didn't respond at first, but then he found the breath to ask: "What are you?"

"I am what I am, Benjamin, just as you are what you are. I go where I am called. Time and space mean nothing to me. I do my job until my job is done and then I move on."

"You're not insane, you're the devil."

"Well, I go by many names, Benjamin. You can call me whatever will make you feel better in the morning. But you have a choice to make and that's completely on you."

"What if I don't make a choice?"

The old man sighed as if he had heard this one a million times. "Choosing not to choose is still making a choice, Benjamin."

The sheriff lowered his head, studied the pine needles and leaves on the ground, and then raised his head again, his eyes full of fresh tears.

"Paul, I love you," Sheriff Logan said, shifting his arm, squeezing the trigger, and shooting his son in his chest.

Paul took two steps backwards, the rifle slipping from his hands. He fell and landed on his back, his eyes locked on the swirling dark clouds above, and he did not move.

The old man watched as another white light exploded across the land.

34.

BEN AWOKE IN THE MIDDLE of the night, but he didn't kick or scream or experience any of the usual spontaneous reactions to one of his PTSD nightmares. As far as he could recall, it had been a dreamless sleep.

Jennifer was curled up behind him, holding on tight to protect him from whatever demons might come searching for him in the dark, just like she always did.

She hadn't awoken at all, and Ben slid out from under her arm and left the room, moving to the bedrooms of their sleeping children.

He stood outside Paul's door for a moment. He hadn't checked on his kids in the night since they were little, but he turned the knob anyway and opened the door a crack. Paul was asleep in his bed, snoring lightly.

He checked on Mary next—his not-so-little girl was snug under the covers, holding a stuffed giraffe to her chest—and then he closed the door and walked downstairs.

Once he reached the first floor, he made himself a cup of coffee and stepped out onto the front porch. The air above the mountains burst to life with bright colors around the rising sun, mostly red and orange and some purple, and the lack of clouds promised a morning of crisp blue sky.

Ben had a feeling it was going to be a beautiful day.

35.

THE OLD MAN STEADIED HIMSELF with his cane, regaining his bearings. He won some and he lost some, that was true, but he hated losing very much.

The night was dark and the stars overhead burned brightly. There were no city lights. The old man stood on a cobblestone road. He almost always started out on a road or path, whether it be pavement or concrete or pressed sand or packed dirt.

As he had told Sheriff Logan, time and space were mere words to him. He never knew how long he might spend in one place or where he might travel to next. Or *when* he might arrive there.

The old man gazed at the stars and determined he had journeyed to Europe in July 1919. Germany, to be exact.

The old man began walking, carrying his cane and occasionally twirling it. There was a young man he wanted to meet. A young man with great potential. This young man was merely a *Verbindungsmann*, an intelligence agent, but his secret dream was much, much grander than that. This young man could really go places and do big, big things if someone with a little power did him a favor or two.

The old man smiled as he walked and his gray eyes changed colors, as they sometimes did.

The morning sun broke through the trees lining the road, and the old man's smile turned into a grin.

It would be a beautiful day, and there was much for him to do.

BONUS STORIES

THE MEEK SHALL INHERIT...

BY RICHARD CHIZMAR

"WOULD YOU EAT A DOG turd for a hundred bucks?"

Brian stopped mid-shot, the basketball poised above his head. He looked over at his friend standing in the driveway. "Dry turd or fresh and wet?"

Jimmy considered the question and answered with a crooked smile, "Moist. Couple hours old."

Brian dribbled to the baseline and shot. *Swish.* He gathered the loose ball and drilled a pass into Jimmy's scrawny chest. "Make it or you're the horse. Again."

Jimmy dribbled awkwardly to the baseline. Started to shoot.

"Back up, you little cheater."

Jimmy flipped his best friend the finger and backed up a few steps. Took the shot. *Airball.*

Brian threw his arms in the air and ran around the court, hooting, "Brian Anderson! Champion of the worrrrld!"

Jimmy shook his head and kicked the ball into the front yard. "Dick sucking champion of the world."

Out on the street, a muscular, bare-chested teenager cruised by on a skateboard. He glanced at the two boys standing in the driveway and smirked. "You girls having fun playing kickball?"

Jimmy took a step toward the road. "Your mom had fun playing with my—"

Brian came up behind him, clamped a hand over his friend's mouth, silencing him in mid-insult.

But it was too late.

The muscle-head on the skateboard grinded to a stop. "What was that?"

"He was talking to me," Brian said. "Not you, Billy."

Brian squeezed Jimmy's shoulder, and Jimmy got the hint. "Ow. Yeah, I wasn't talking to you."

Billy glared at them for a moment, deciding whether they were worth the trouble. He looked up and down the street—most bullies, Brian believed, had a kind of grown-up radar—and then, he gave them the double-bird and pushed off down the street.

Brian sat down in the grassy front yard and let out a deep breath. "Jesus, Jimmy, you and your big mouth."

Jimmy plopped down next to him. "I think we could take him."

"I think you're wrong."

"He's not that tough."

"He's fifteen. We're twelve. He smokes and has arms the size of our legs. We still have sleepovers."

Jimmy shrugged. "Nothing wrong with sleepovers. They're fun."

Brian couldn't argue with that, so he laid back and stared at the passing clouds overhead. Jimmy plucked blades of grass and flicked them into the air, one after the other. Somewhere down the street, a dog barked.

Jimmy finally broke the silence. "This sucks. Second week of summer vacation and we're already bored."

"At least you were at the lake all last week," Brian said, squinting at a cloud that resembled an alligator.

"Yeah, with my mom and dad. Like that's any fun. Do you have any idea how much sunscreen my Mom makes me wear?"

Brian laughed. He did have an idea. He had seen it many times firsthand at the neighborhood swimming pool. When Jimmy's mom was finished with him, Jimmy looked like a skinny, little Yeti ready to prowl a snowy mountaintop.

"And my Dad...did you know he still wears a Speedo?"

Brian belly-laughed. He couldn't help it.

"Not funny, dude. It's freaking embarrassing. You can practically see his junk."

Thinking about Mr. Gallagher's junk was not a pretty picture. Jimmy's old man weighed about three hundred pounds—and that was naked. How he had produced a beanpole of a son (that's what he always called Jimmy) was a mystery to everyone.

Brian shook away the disturbing image, sat up and patted Jimmy on the back. "C'mon, let's play another game of Horse."

Jimmy groaned and pushed himself to his feet just as a van slowed out on the road and swung into the driveway next door. The boys watched a middle-aged man, tall and thin, bald and wearing thick glasses, get out of the van and walk toward the house.

"Hi, Mr. Pruitt," Jimmy yelled, waving.

The man flinched, like he had been woken from a daydream, and looked over at the boys. He opened his mouth like he was going to say something, then closed it again and gave them a shy wave before disappearing into the front door.

"That was weird," Brian said.

Jimmy nodded, still staring at the closed front door. "He's been like that for awhile now. My mom says it's because he's still in mourning."

"Didn't Mrs. Pruitt die like a year ago?"

Jimmy shrugged. "My mom says it takes a long time, especially when you've been together for so many years." And, just like that, Jimmy was thinking about Mrs. Pruitt's kind face and her sweet voice and her chocolate chip cookies—and he felt his eyes filling up.

"You okay, man?" Brian asked.

Jimmy turned away, wiping at his eyes. "I'm fine. It's just sad, that's all. I feel sorry for him."

"Me, too."

"I don't ever want to get married," Jimmy said.

"No worries there, retard. What chick is gonna be dumb enough to marry your ugly ass?"

Jimmy was bright enough in the ways of childhood to understand the twelve-year-old translation of this insult was: *it's all gonna be okay, buddy*—so he returned the favor.

"Plenty...starting with your sister."

Brian tackled him and the two boys rolled around in the front yard, laughing and wrestling, until Jimmy's mom poked her head out the front door a few minutes later and called Jimmy inside for dinner.

LATER THAT evening, a June thunderstorm swept in from the North, turning curbside gutters into miniature rapids and knocking out electricity for most of the town, including both sides of Jimmy's street.

By ten o'clock the next morning, the storm had cleared out, the sky was a brilliant, robin-egg blue, and the electric was back up and running at Jimmy's house.

Jimmy and Brian sat across from each other on the front porch. Half-finished glasses of lemonade and stacks of baseball cards covered the small table, which sat between them. After an hour of intense bargaining (arguing) about fair trades, both boys were slumped back in plastic patio chairs, staring at the screens of their cell-phones.

"Damn it," Jimmy moaned and tossed his phone onto the table, knocking over a pile of cards. "I'm getting tired of Hearthstone."

Brian looked up from his phone. "That's because you suck at Hearthstone."

Jimmy ignored the dig and sat up in his chair, an uncharacteristically serious look on his face. "Can I tell you something?"

Brian recognized the tone of his friend's voice and knew it was something important. The last time he'd heard that tone of voice was when Jimmy confided in him about seeing Jan Thompson changing into a bathing suit through her bedroom window. He was eleven then.

Brian turned off his game. "Sure, what's up?"

"You promise not to laugh?"

Brian shrugged. "I promise to try not to. What's going on, man?"

Jimmy looked over his left shoulder at the house, and then over his right at the front yard. Seemingly content that no one was eavesdropping, he scooted his chair closer to Brian. Lowered his voice. "You remember what we were talking about yesterday...about Mr. Pruitt?"

"About him being sad?"

Jimmy shook his head. "About him being different, acting weird."

"Okay, yeah."

Jimmy looked over his shoulder again in the direction of his next-door neighbor's house, then back at Brian. "I was thinking about it last night...remembering *things*." He took a deep breath. "I think something bad might be going on over there."

"What exactly does *something bad* mean?" Brian slid his chair a little closer.

Jimmy thought about it for a moment before answering. "You promised you wouldn't laugh."

"Just tell me what you—"

"I think Mr. Pruitt might be a serial killer."

Brian laughed in his friend's face, then immediately regretted it as he watched Jimmy's cheeks flush beet-red in anger and embarrassment.

"You promised!" Jimmy hissed, jumping to his feet and heading off the porch.

Brian chased after him. "I promised to *try* not to laugh, and I couldn't help it. I'm sorry, man, but Mr. Pruitt a serial killer? That's just nutty."

Jimmy spun on him, his eyes darting all around the yard. "Keep your voice down."

Brian whispered, "Okay, okay, I'm sorry."

"C'mon." Jimmy led Brian across the still-wet front lawn, away from the house, to the curb, where they sat side by side, their bare feet resting in the slow-trickling run-off that still flowed down the street toward a distant sewer grate.

Jimmy sat there silently, pouting, staring down at the ground. He flicked a pebble on the road with his big toe. Cleared his throat. Coughed. Finally, he looked up at Brian and said, "I've seen things. Heard things."

"*Things...*" Brian said. "Like the time you thought you saw a UFO landing in the woods behind the park? Or the time you thought you saw the librarian from school holding up a bank on the evening news?"

"The lady in the security video looked just like her and—"

Brian put out his hands in surrender. "All I'm saying is that you watch a lot of movies and have a big imagination and tell a lot of crazy stories." He glanced at the house next door. "Mr. Pruitt is a cool guy. Remember when he helped us fix our go-cart? And when he bought all our lemonade when no one else was even slowing down to take a look?"

"I know he's a nice guy, Brian."

"How about when he covered for us to your parents the night we were bombing cars with snowballs? He saved our asses."

"Look, I know Mr. Pruitt has always been nice to us. But my mom is right—he's changed since his wife died."

"So what, he's quiet now, keeps to himself, maybe he's a little weird. Doesn't make him a serial killer."

"I've heard screams over there."

Brian looked closely at his friend. "Screams?"

Jimmy nodded. "Couple of times. Last week when you were at the lake."

"And you're sure?"

Jimmy nodded again. "First time, I was raking grass in the back yard and I wasn't a hundred percent sure what I'd heard. But the next evening, I was back there shooting my BB gun and I heard it again. I'm sure."

"Okay, what else?"

"The van."

"What about it?"

"What does an old guy like that need with a van? I mean, why trade in a perfectly good Cadillac for a van when you're all alone?"

Brian shrugged. "Maybe the Cadillac reminded him too much of his wife."

"And he's been shopping a lot. Every day he brings home something new."

"So what?"

"What's he need with a video camera and a tripod? I watched him haul in two metal cages another day. What's he need cages for?"

"Maybe he bought a dog."

"Must be the kind of dog that never needs to go outside then."

Brian rolled his eyes. "What else, Sherlock?"

"The night before you came home, I was helping my dad lay down mulch in the front yard when Mr. Pruitt came home. He'd backed the van into the driveway and was unloading something into his carport, so my dad sent me over there to help. But he didn't want my help. He acted all nervous and pretty much shooed my ass outta there. But I saw some of what he was unloading..."

"What was it?"

"I didn't really know at first. It was all these big sheets of insulation and big foam panels and boxes of sealant and glue." Jimmy, dead serious, locked his eyes on his friend's face. "I looked it up on the internet later that night...I had memorized the exact brands I saw on the boxes. It was all material for sound-proofing a room."

Brian looked down at the wet pavement, his mind turning. He knew Jimmy liked to tell stories, he always had, but he also knew Jimmy was the smartest kid in the entire middle school.

"What do you think?" Jimmy prodded.

Brian looked up at his friend. "I think I should spend the night at your house tonight—and we should keep a close eye on Mr. Pruitt's house."

"BE QUIET or he's gonna hear us," Jimmy whispered.

"He's not even home, dork. How's he gonna hear us?"

"Oh, yeah."

Despite the serious nature of their investigation, both boys giggled as they crawled on their bellies along the side of Mr. Pruitt's house. It was dusk now. Fireflies blinked in the coming darkness. Crickets chirped their night symphony in the tall grass. A hush lay over the neighborhood.

As the morning had passed into afternoon, and afternoon into evening, the boys' moods had lightened. They spent the majority of the day playing whiffle-ball in the park with their friends and watching high school girls in short-shorts and tank-tops playing Frisbee.

They'd been disappointed to discover that Mr. Pruitt hadn't returned home when they'd first come outside after dinner. To pass the time, they'd gone back in the house and watched the first three innings of the Orioles game with Jimmy's father in the den. Once it was dark enough, they'd told Jimmy's dad that they were going to the store for ice cream and were once again disappointed to not find Mr. Pruitt's van parked in his driveway or carport.

Instead of waiting any longer, they'd decided to take advantage of his absence and investigate his ground-level basement windows. Brian led the way, slithering flat on his stomach like a snake, just a dozen or so feet away from the first window, with Jimmy right behind him. For both boys, it felt a lot like playing Army when they were younger.

"Ugh...I think I just put my elbow in dog crap," Jimmy whined.

Brian giggled softly. "Maybe Mr. Pruitt got that dog after all."

"Oh, shut up."

They both shut up and kept crawling.

After another minute, Brian looked back over his shoulder and asked, "What're we gonna say if your dad looks out the window and sees us?"

"That's easy. We say we're looking for toads in the window wells. Remember how we used to collect 'em in buckets?"

"Sometimes I actually forget that you're so smart. Almost there..."

Brian crawled another few feet and stopped—and let out a quiet gasp. Jimmy crawled around him and halted at his side, leaning up on his elbows for a better look.

The narrow basement window had been blacked out. It was hard to tell in the shadows, but it looked like someone had taken thick black tape and covered the inside of the glass with it. Whatever it was, you definitely couldn't see through it.

"Believe me now?" Jimmy whispered.

"WAKE UP."

Brian went on snoring. Jimmy poked his friend in the ribs again, harder this time. "C'mon, wake up."

Brian groaned and rolled onto his side. "Lemme alone."

"He's home," Jimmy whispered and crawled to the window.

Brian sat up in his sleeping bag on the floor. "What time is it?"

"Almost midnight. He just pulled in. Hurry up."

Brian kicked his way out of the sleeping bag and, rubbing his eyes, joined his friend at the window. "What's he doing?"

"Nothing yet. He's still in the van."

They watched in silence, their faces pressed close to the window. Mr. Pruitt's lawn and driveway were lost in a spider-web of shadows.

"You sure he's still in there?" Brian asked.

Before Jimmy could answer, the driver's-side door opened, the van's interior light flashed on, and the boys had a clear view of Mr. Pruitt stepping out onto the driveway. He closed the door with a muffled *thud* and the night swallowed him.

Brian shifted for a better look and bumped his head against the window.

"Be careful," Jimmy whispered. "He could hear us."

"I can't see him. Did he go inside?"

"I never saw the front door open. Maybe he went in the side door under the carport."

"Or maybe he's sneaking over here right now for a closer look at us," Brian teased. "And he's wearing a clown mask and carrying a butcher knife."

Jimmy punched his friend in the shoulder. "That's not funny."

"Hey, there he is," Brian whispered, pointing out the window.

A narrow slice of dim light appeared at the back of the van. The boys squinted into the shadows and could just make out the bottom half of Mr. Pruitt's legs; the upper half of his body was blocked by the open rear door.

"What's he doing?" Jimmy asked.

"Getting something out of the back of the van I think."

"I told you, didn't I? I told you—"

The door closed with another *thud* and even though the driveway was thrown back into shadow, the boys' eyes had adjusted to the dark well enough for them to catch a glimpse—

—of Mr. Pruitt disappearing into the carport, carrying a large burlap sack over his shoulder. The sack was moving in jerks and fits, as if whatever was trapped inside was struggling to get out.

"ARE YOU crazy? We can't call the police. Not yet."

It was the next morning, and a sleep-deprived Jimmy was pacing on his front porch. His mother had made the boys a breakfast of scrambled eggs and bacon and toast, and taken off for a day of shopping with one of her girlfriends. The boys had the house to themselves for the rest of the morning and afternoon.

"What do you mean, *not yet*?" Brian asked, watching his friend stroll back and forth like one of those sick tigers you always saw at the zoo. "He could've had a little kid in that sack."

"Do you have any idea what my father will do to me if we call the police on Mr. Pruitt and we're wrong? I'll be grounded for the rest of the summer."

"Now we're *wrong*? You're the one who was so sure. You even have me half-convinced!"

Jimmy stopped pacing. Walked over to his friend. "Listen, we're not wrong. Something weird is going on over there. We just have to figure out what it is before we tell my parents or call the police."

"And how we gonna do that?"

Jimmy tilted his head in a way that Brian immediately recognized as trouble.

"Oh, shit, I know that look."

Jimmy smiled. His face was pale and drawn, but his eyes were bright. "Mr. Pruitt never comes home for lunch. Ever. We're in and out in ten minutes."

Brian groaned. "I knew it."

"We empty our pockets beforehand. Nothing we might leave behind on accident. Yes, I learned that from a movie. I'll set the timer on my watch. Ten minutes and we're gone, no matter what."

"How we getting in? The doors will be locked."

Jimmy pulled two objects out of the back pocket of his jeans: a small screwdriver and a laminated *GameStop* membership card.

"Your Uncle Manny?" Brian asked, eyebrows raised.

Manny was Jimmy's dad's black-sheep younger brother. He talked too loud, drank too much, and had actually done time when he was barely in his twenties. He was firecrackers and magic tricks and dirty jokes. A big kid with a heart of gold.

Jimmy smiled that tired smile of his and nodded. "Good old Uncle Manny."

"HE PROMISED to show me how to hot-wire a car one day, too. He said it's a lot harder than in the movies."

Brian stood behind his friend at Mr. Pruitt's back door, glancing anxiously over his shoulder. "Just hurry the hell up, will ya?"

"The key is to not leave any marks on the door frame, in case you have to come back later." Jimmy carefully wedged the screwdriver in a little further and jiggled it up and down.

"We ain't coming back later."

"I know that, just saying." He held the screwdriver in place with his left hand and removed the card from his pocket with his other hand. He aligned the card between the wooden door-frame and the metal latch, then started swiping it up and down. After a moment, he stopped and wiped his hand on his jeans. "Sweaty. Guess I'm nervous."

"That makes two of us," Brian said. "Hey, if we're being so careful, why aren't we wearing gloves or something?"

"Don't need 'em. It gets to the point where cops are over here lifting fingerprints, we're screwed anyway."

The thought made Brian even more nervous. "We should just give it up, man. It's not gonna work."

There was an audible *click*—and the door swung inward a few inches. They caught a glimpse of linoleum floor inside.

Jimmy looked back at his friend. "You were saying?"

"Oh, shut up."

Jimmy stuffed the screwdriver and membership card back into his pocket, carefully nudged the door open, and stepped inside. Brian followed right behind him and started to close the door.

"Leave it open. In case we have to make a quick escape."

"Lemme guess...you saw it in a movie?"

"As a matter of fact, I did."

"Jesus," Brian said, looking around. "What's that smell?"

They were standing in Mr. Pruitt's kitchen, and it was a mess. Dirty dishes were stacked in the sink and on the surrounding countertop. Empty pizza and Chinese food delivery boxes littered the kitchen table and overflowed from the trashcan. There was a pile of old newspapers stacked in front of the dishwasher.

"I have a bad feeling about this," Jimmy whispered.

Brian, eyes wide, nodded in agreement.

"The smell is coming from down there," Jimmy said, motioning to a door in the adjoining hallway.

"Basement?"

Jimmy nodded and headed that way.

"I was afraid you were gonna say that," Brian said, following.

"I used to come down here every Christmas Eve when I was little to see Mr. Pruitt's train-set."

Jimmy opened the door into complete darkness. He gathered his courage and slid his hand along the wall just inside the doorway until he found the light switch and flipped it on. The stairway was long and narrow and covered in the same ugly shade of gold carpeting Jimmy remembered from years past.

"After you," Brian said, his voice cracking.

They slowly started down the stairs—and both boys heard and smelled the animals before they actually saw them.

"What the hell is that?" Jimmy asked, and then they reached the bottom of the stairway and turned the corner.

The room erupted in a cacophony of frantic barking and growling and whining as soon as the boys walked into view.

The entire length of one wall was lined with small cages. There had to be twenty or more of them. Each secured with a heavy padlock. Inside the metal cages were mostly dogs and cats. But there were also squirrels and rabbits and even a raccoon. And positioned along the adjoining wall, underneath one of the blacked-out basement windows, were two large, clear-plastic hutches, each containing a monkey. The wiry monkeys skittered from one side of their enclosures to the other, eyes bugging, clawing madly to get out.

Jimmy stood a few feet from the bottom of the stairway, his mind racing to register what his eyes were seeing. The smell was horrible here in the closed room; a toxic mixture of piss and crap and something chemical he could almost taste on his tongue. The basement walls were soundproofed.

"Some serial killer!" Brian said from behind him in a booming voice. He walked deeper into the room, laughing with relief. "Old Man Pruitt is Doctor Doolittle!"

"Sometimes they start by torturing animals," Jimmy said, his words almost drowned out by the animal screeches. "Then they move on to people."

Brian pointed out a stainless steel table—with leather straps—in the far corner of the basement. Syringes and vials of what looked like medicine were lined up on a nearby shelf. "Looks like he's trying to help them, not torture them."

Jimmy glanced in the opposite corner of the room, noticed a computer, its monitor-screen glowing, sitting on a small desk next to a printer. He headed that way.

Behind him, Brian bent down and reached his hand through one of the cages. A mangy cocker-spaniel gently licked his fingers. "Poor little guy. All cramped up in there." He got to his feet and studied several of the other cages. "Helping or not, they shouldn't be locked up like this. Most of them don't even have water."

Jimmy stopped in front of the desk. Reached out and nudged the mouse, and the screen-saver image of a sunny beach disappeared and was replaced by a series of strange letters and numbers. He leaned closer, trying to remember where he had seen something similar.

"Hey, Jimmy," Brian said from behind him. "Wonder what the suit's for?"

He looked over and saw Brian struggling to hold up a full-body suit, the heavy-duty kind you see astronauts wearing on television. A helmet with a clear faceplate hung from a hook on the wall next to him.

"Beats me. Just put it back, man." Jimmy returned his attention to the computer screen, once again searching his memory for where he'd seen such writing.

"I bet these keys are for the cages," Brian said, but Jimmy, lost in deep thought, didn't hear him. His eyes and nose stung from the horrible stench; his brain hurt from thinking. He was about to give up when the answer suddenly came to him like a ship sailing free of a fogbank. He snapped his fingers.

"It's Arabic! I remember it from school." He scrolled down, then clicked on a blurry photo at the bottom of the computer screen—and almost screamed when something brushed against his pants leg.

He looked down and saw a flash of black cat. He turned back to his friend and frowned. "What are you doing?"

Loose dogs and cats scampered across the basement and up the stairs to freedom. As Jimmy watched, Brian flung open another cage door and lifted a fat rabbit onto the floor below. The rabbit hopped in a drunk circle, then raced away, joining the others. "What's it look like I'm doing?" He laughed and moved on to the next cage.

Jimmy opened his mouth to protest, but before he could, screaming erupted from the computer behind him. Startled, he spun around and realized that a video was playing on the monitor:

A dark-skinned man wearing a filthy robe sat strapped to a chair in the middle of a small room. He screamed and wailed and fought against his restraints to no avail. Harsh voices could be heard off-screen speaking in a foreign language. After another thirty seconds of screaming, a scraggly mutt limped on-screen. The man stopped screaming and started crying. The dog wagged its tail and licked the man's restrained hands. The man started screaming again and tried to jerk away, but before long the screams were drowned out by a deep guttural choking sound. The camera zoomed in on the man's face, and Jimmy could see blood and bile spilling from the man's mouth in a foamy mess. And then his eyes erupted in twin geysers of blood that dribbled down his cheeks, and after a few more seconds, the man went limp and quiet. The foreign voice spoke up again, and then someone shuffled on-screen wearing a heavy-duty suit eerily similar to the one hanging on the wall right there in the basement.

The puzzle pieces suddenly snapped into place inside Jimmy's brain and his entire body went rigid with terror. "Brian..." All of a sudden, he wished he had brought his cellphone. He wished it more than anything else in the world. "Brian...STOP!"

Brian was kneeling in front of the second monkey enclosure. The first hutch was empty, the door wide open. "Why? I feel sorry for 'em, Jimmy."

Jimmy's voice was thick with surging fear. "He might not be a serial killer, but I think Mr. Pruitt is working with some very bad people."

Brian pulled the open lock from the latch and tossed it to the floor beside him. "What kind of bad people?"

"Like ISIS-terrorist-bad people."

Brian rolled his eyes. "Dude, you've seen too many movies. Mr. Pruitt's an old man. He's up to some weird shit down here, but he's as American as you and me."

"I don't think so," Jimmy said, his legs feeling like rubber. "Not anymore."

Brian yanked open the glass door and the brown monkey skittered into his arms.

"Brian, don't..."

Brian, still down on a knee in front of the hutch, grinned and cradled the monkey in his arms like a baby. "Look how cute he is!" He pressed his face close to the monkey's tiny head. "You're so cute. Yes, you are. You're so darn..."

The words suddenly stopped—and Brian's voice faded to a wet gargle. The monkey slipped from his arms and scampered happily away. Brian didn't move, just kept staring down at his lap, his long hair obscuring his face.

Jimmy backed up a step. "You okay, man?"

He didn't answer.

Jimmy backed up another step. "Brian...?"

Brian slowly lifted his head, looked up at his friend. His eyes were bleeding. Dark foam bubbled from his open mouth. He rose up and reached out for Jimmy, took a zombie-like step forward, and then he collapsed to the ground face-first, convulsing.

Jimmy stood there, frozen, watching his friend die. Everything made sense now—*the animals, the vials, the chemical smell, the Hazmat suit*—and nothing made sense at all. He thought about his mother and father and his Uncle Manny, and he turned and sprinted for the stairs.

He was almost to the top of the staircase when he felt something small and heavy latch onto his back with an ear-piercing screech. Sharp claws dug into his back, and he felt the brush of bristly fur against his neck.

He staggered into the kitchen, flailing, trying to wrestle the beast off of him. Even in his panic, he noticed the dogs and cats fleeing outside through the open kitchen door, scattering in the yard and running off in all directions. Free again.

His frantic mind chose that moment to flash another scene from a movie and even amidst the chaos, it bothered him that he couldn't remember the title: *Common house-pets carrying a dangerous new strain of rabies. Infected people going violently insane before dying agonizing deaths. Then, finally...the end of the world.*

Jimmy slammed his back against the kitchen wall, trying to shake the beast loose. He knocked piles of dishes to the floor where they shattered into pieces. He kicked over the pile of newspapers. The beast only screeched its awful banshee cry and dug its claws deeper into Jimmy's scalp.

He stumbled out the door into the back yard and felt the sun hit his tear-stained face. Its comforting warmth and blinding brightness filled his final moment of consciousness before the monkey lunged and buried its razor-sharp teeth deep in the flesh of Jimmy's neck.

And then his throat was closing up like a caved-in mine-shaft and he couldn't breathe; and his skin felt like it had been set ablaze; and hot blood poured from his eyes in twin rivulets—and then he felt and saw nothing at all.

WHAT THEY LEFT BEHIND

BY BRIAN JAMES FREEMAN

SCOTT SODERMAN STOOD IN THE open dock door as rain pounded the parking lot and the forest beyond. Trailers full of pallets waited their turn at the other doors. Below the loading docks were two enormous storm drains, both of them clogged with leaves, brush, and debris that had collected during the years the Timlico complex sat abandoned. Dirty water pooled like a lake.

By the entrance to the parking lot, next to what remained of the chain-link fence, was the ancient *For Sale* sign, tattered and faded with age. A hopeful and bright *Sold!* banner was nailed across the front.

Scott's father had bought this dump as his last ditch effort to keep the family's logistics business afloat in the new economy, but the odds were not looking good in Scott's opinion. Timlico was the name of the company that had originally built this warehouse, along with the attached office building and the enormous factory around back. The property had been deteriorating for years, sitting unoccupied since the sudden closure of the entire corporation. The remnants of the complex were rotting and rusting within the vine-covered walls, but the warehouse was still solid. It was made of steel and concrete and sheet metal, which could endure the ravages of time better than drywall and carpet—although nothing man-made could last forever. Given enough time, Mother Nature would reclaim all of this land.

"What a way to spend a Saturday," Scott whispered.

A voice behind him replied: "Yeah, the storm's getting worse."

Scott jumped and spun around as George stepped onto the loading dock.

"Jesus H. Christ, don't sneak up on me!" Scott said, clutching at his heart like an old man. "If you kill me, I'm pretty sure my sister will have to dump you, dude. And my dad will probably fire your ass."

George laughed. He was a few years older than Scott and he had grown up in some town in New Jersey that no one in the Soderman family had ever heard of before he started dating Scott's sister.

George said, "Sorry about that. Thought you heard me coming."

"Now I need a smoke. Got a light?" Scott asked, pulling a pack of cigarettes from his pocket. His lighter was in the car and he felt no desire to brave the storm to retrieve it.

"Nada. Those things will kill you before you're fifty," George said.

"If I live that long." Scott laughed at his own joke and put the pack of cigarettes back in his pocket for later. "They calm my nerves."

"If you say so."

"I do. And there's not much I can actually do here. I may as well get busy getting cancer."

"So why'd you volunteer then?"

"I would have been dragged along one way or another so I volunteered before my father could draft me."

George laughed. "Like the Army."

"Yeah, like the Army."

"I just wish we had two more weeks to get everything ready for this move. We're trying to get too much done this weekend, mistakes are bound to happen."

"I guess there wasn't much choice," Scott said. "We're getting evicted from the old building on Monday, right?"

"Correctamundo. Good thing we got this place for dirt cheap."

"You guys are planning to demolish the office building and the factory, right?"

"That's the plan. We only need the warehouse and we agreed to tear the other sections down since they'll never be up to code again. That's how we got such a great deal. Why?"

"Don't tell anyone, but I want to check everything out before it's gone. You know, try to find something neat that was left behind by the previous owners. A souvenir of sorts. It'll be cool."

George laughed again. "If you say so, Scott."

Mary Soderman was operating the forklift and she sped by her boyfriend and her brother, sounding the horn as she passed, although they had heard her coming a mile away. She was busy unloading pallets and crates from the trailers lined up at the dock doors. Scott and George had one shared responsibility: tracking the inventory to make sure each delivery was recorded properly.

Every hour a truck driver brought another full trailer from the old warehouse where Scott's father and the rest of the full-time employees were busy closing down operations. The driver then returned one of the empty trailers to the other side of town and the process repeated itself again and again. It would have been a tough day even without the storm.

Mary stopped the forklift a few feet from where Scott and George stood watching the rain. The yellow machine's weary engine growled like some kind of hungry beast. The battered forklift had seen better days and the heavy scent of oil and grease emanated from under the hood.

Mary shouted: "Dad called and said the power went out at the old warehouse. There's a good chance it'll happen here, too, so someone needs to check the generator."

"Okay, I'll go," Scott said.

"Take this." Mary tossed a flashlight to her brother. "And watch yourself in there. You don't want to fall through any holes in the floor. Why don't you go with him, George? Make sure he gets back in one piece."

Mary gunned the forklift's engine and rolled into a trailer to grab the next pallet, leaving a cloud of black smoke hanging in her wake. There was no time for chitchat. A lot of work needed to get done this weekend.

George and Scott made their way across the warehouse to the double doors that served as a gateway to the offices. Tacked onto the wall was a map of the complex, and at first glance the lines on the oversized paper resembled a giant maze, but the color code system helped bring some order to the chaos.

"The generator should be in the basement under the offices," George said.

"Looks like the stairs are on the other side of the building," Scott replied, pointing at a tiny square labeled MECHANICAL ROOM #7/BASEMENT ACCESS. "It's a straight shot."

"Okay, let's go. I don't want to spend too long in there."

"Scared of the dark?"

"Don't ask."

"Too late."

They opened the double doors and stared into the pitch-black void while Scott swatted around the wall, finding mold and wetness and eventually a series of switches. He flipped them. Some of the lights flickered to life, but not many.

"Holy crap," Scott whispered.

The hallway was eerily cloaked in shadows, but he could see the mess well enough: piles of discarded paperwork, water stained ceiling tiles that were crumbling and falling onto the damp carpet, and colorful graffiti on the walls.

"Watch your step," George said as they started down the hallway.

Scott used the flashlight to guide them through the wide gaps of gloom where the overhead lights were broken or burned out, but he stopped at the first office with an open door so he could look inside.

A high-backed chair was overturned behind the metal desk, a framed aerial photograph of the property was smashed on the floor, and two filing cabinets were stripped of their drawers. Paperwork, discarded beer cans, used condoms, and crumpled fast food bags littered the office. A steady stream of dirty water dripped from a yellowed ceiling tile in the far corner.

"What a fun place," Scott said as he and George started walking again. "I can see why you're going to bulldoze it."

Dozens of offices and conference rooms and numerous hallways branched off to their left and right. If there had been any twists and turns along the route to their destination, they surely would have gotten lost for hours.

"Why'd they leave all this stuff?" George asked, pointing at another filing cabinet tipped on its side. Yellowed and wet piles of paperwork covered the floor. "I mean, why didn't Timlico take it with them when they closed up shop?"

"Shit, you don't know, do you?"

"Know what?"

"There was a freak fire here about ten years ago. Some people were killed and the company closed because of the lawsuits. There was no reason to take anything with them, I guess."

"How many people?"

"Nearly fifty."

"Jesus, how?"

Scott pointed the beam of the flashlight at a MagCard slot next to a closed office door. "See these panels?"

"Yeah?"

"The doors worked on an electronic passcard system, but when the fire started in the basement, the computer system froze. A bunch of people got trapped in their offices while the smoke was sucked through the ventilation ducts. They didn't burn, they suffocated."

"Jesus Christ. How'd the fire start?"

"Some kind of freak accident," Scott said. "A spark where there shouldn't have been one or something like that. I was just a kid so I don't really remember."

"Damn, this place is creepy," George muttered.

They had reached the end of the hallway where the door marked MECHANICAL ROOM #7/BASEMENT ACCESS—RESTRICTED ACCESS awaited them. Looking back, Scott agreed with George's assessment: the building *was* seriously creepy.

"Like something from a low budget horror flick," he said, trying to sound like he was making a joke. Thinking of the people who had died here made the hallways and trashed offices feel much more sinister than he had expected.

"This might have been a bad idea."

"Do you want to go back? I can handle it myself," Scott said, even though the building really was more disturbing than he had expected. The debris. The sagging ceiling tiles. The wet floors. The maze of hallways. All the lonely offices full of unfinished business. The empty conference rooms where meetings in progress never concluded. Everything they had left behind.

George said: "No, let's just get it done."

Scott opened the door to reveal a narrow set of concrete stairs leading down to another door. He and George exchanged a look, but they said nothing as they descended, both of them gripping the rusted railing tighter than they would ever admit. When they arrived at the bottom of the stairs, Scott tugged on that metal door's heavy handle. The hinges squealed from disuse as the door slowly opened toward him, and he reached inside and found a light switch, which he flipped.

"Damn," Scott muttered as several random and yellowed fluorescent bulbs in the basement sparked to life.

The room was much larger than he had expected. There were hundreds of steel posts supporting the office building above them. Dozens of pipes and ducts crisscrossed the ceiling. There were several wooden benches and metal lockers for the maintenance crew. Most of the lockers were hanging open and a few still had moldy clothing inside. Beyond that were rows full of old desks, filing cabinets, and conference tables, enough to start a dozen companies with, maybe more. And beyond those was a graveyard of forgotten office equipment including hundreds of ancient computers, printers, and copiers Timlico had held onto for some reason.

There was also water on the floor. A lot of water.

Six inches deep on this side of the room, at least, and even deeper on the other side where metal steps led up to a landing with a door marked GENERATOR ROOM. The waterline along the lockers lining the wall to their left showed the difference easily, but the difference didn't make a lot of sense.

"Maybe the floor is sloped?" George suggested.

"Could be." Scott wanted to turn back, but how would he explain that to his sister? They didn't check on the generator because they got scared of the dark? There was some spooky water on the floor? He'd never hear the end of it, not if he lived to be a hundred. "I think we can handle a little water. Let's get this done."

They hurried across the room, the water rising to their knees even though they didn't feel any real grade to the floor. Soon they were slipping on rotting papers and other things they couldn't see below the slimy surface. Doors to their right were marked with notices such as *DANGER! AIR COMPRESSION UNITS* and *WARNING! BOILER* and *MAIN ELECTRICAL SYSTEM CONTROLS*.

Scott and George were still a dozen yards from the stairs to the generator room when the few working overhead lights died without warning.

"Shit," Scott muttered. He lifted the flashlight, shining it on George.

"Let's go back," George whispered. "I hate the dark."

"Why didn't you say that when I asked?"

"I didn't know it would be *this* dark!"

"The generator room isn't much further," Scott said, pointing the light at the stairs. "Let's get the generator started and then we'll haul ass out of here. We'll be quick."

George didn't look convinced, but he started moving again anyway. Scott did his best to keep the narrow circle of light focused on the door, to keep his eyes on their goal, but something was wrong. The air was growing colder as the water got deeper.

There was a splash behind them and Scott stopped dead in his tracks. He whirled around, waving the flashlight high and low and left and right, but he saw nothing.

"Let's get out of here," George whispered.

The air had grown even colder and Scott's teeth involuntarily chattered as he searched the room with the flashlight again.

From the darkness came an anguished moan. Then there was another. And then another. Soft at first, then getting louder.

None of the sounds seemed real to Scott. They were there, but they weren't.

Scott opened his mouth to say something to George, but as he drew in a breath, his lungs filled with smoke and he began to cough. The smoke surrounded him, smothering him, and he could barely breath.

"Let's go!" George said, diving forward and swimming toward the stairs just a dozen steps away. Scott followed, coughing and struggling to keep the flashlight out of the water, the circle of light swinging wildly around them.

They climbed the stairs in a panic to the door marked GEN-ERATOR ROOM and they didn't stop until they were safely on the landing. Scott pointed the flashlight back to where the ripples from their panicked swim were still spreading across the water, but there was no smoke and no one to be seen anywhere.

"What the hell was that?" George muttered, his words turning to fog in the increasingly chilly air.

"Just our imaginations," Scott said, forcing a tight laugh. "Our imaginations got away from us. Gotta be!"

"That wasn't my imagination. Something's very wrong here. We need to keep moving. Try the door," George whispered.

Scott did as he was told and the door opened without issue. He had expected a small generator like the one at his father's hunting cabin, but instead he found a control panel that NASA might have used to launch rockets in the '60s. There was also a door on the far side of the room labeled: RESTRICTED AREA! ACCESS TO BACK-UP GENERATORS 1 THRU 5! AUTHORIZED MECHANICS ONLY.

Scott approached the master workstation. The control panel featured gauges and buttons and a few blank screens. None of the controls made much sense without knowledge of the system, but there *was* a green button labeled ON. Scott pushed that button.

Nothing happened. No sputtering. No revving of power. None of the gauge needles even twitched.

"Damn," Scott muttered. "Should have figured as much."

"Broken?" George asked, flipping a few switches as if that might help.

"Something like that. Maybe no fuel. Or maybe I just don't know how to run this thing, ya know?"

"Okay, we tried. Let's get the hell out of here, okay?"

"Works for me," Scott said.

He returned to the door, but then stopped dead in his tracks as fear tightened around his throat like a noose. The stairs were submerged by water that was quickly rising yet that wasn't what made a shriek escape from between Scott's lips before he even knew the sound was coming.

They weren't alone.

Smoke filled the air of the basement, and in the smoke were people moving toward the stairs and the door, their arms flailing above their heads. Forgotten cries and screams bounced off the walls and the foaming water. The people motioned at Scott, calling to him, reaching for him.

"Holy mother of God," George whispered as he grabbed onto Scott's shoulder to steady himself.

Scott pushed George backwards into the generator room and slammed the door shut as hard as he could. The flashlight slipped from his hand. The bulb shattered when it hit the floor and the instant blackness washed over the two men.

"What the hell?" Scott said, his voice cracking. "I mean, seriously, what the fuck!"

Footsteps on the stairs approached the door. The brooding cries grew louder as the pops and crackles of a raging fire roared in the distance.

"I think they're ghosts," George whispered.

"Ghosts aren't real!"

"Maybe you should tell them that."

Scott stared into the pure black nothingness as the harsh shouts continued outside the room. Angry hands pounded on the door, scratched at the doorknob. Hoarse screaming followed. Water slipped under the door and lapped at their shoes. Every rapid beat of Scott's heart was a jackhammer pounding his ribs.

Then came a moment of surreal clarity.

Scott cried out: "I think they're doing whatever they did when they died! I don't think they can hurt us!"

George didn't reply right away. Then:

"We're not alone in here," he whispered.

Scott started to open his mouth, then stopped. George was right. There was someone else in the room. Deliberate, wet footsteps approached them.

Scott heard a distinct *click, click, click*. The sound reminded him of all the times he had played with his lighter, flicking at the sparkwheel, causing the flames to jump again and again and again. *Click, click, click...*

"Scott, what's that?" George asked.

"A butane lighter..." Scott's words died in his throat.

The footsteps were getting closer. There was another series of clicks, then a spark jumped in the darkness. Then another. Then another. Closer and closer and closer.

"We have to get out of here," Scott said, fear consuming him. There was another spark, even closer, and he jumped. He stammered, cleared his throat, and forced the words: "Those things out there, I don't think they can hurt us. But whatever is in here...."

The thought trailed off and he reached for the door without finishing his statement.

"Let's go then, let's go fast," George whispered, directly into Scott's ear, making him jump again.

Together they pulled the door open, stepped out onto the landing and dove over the steps, through the smoke and the screamed memories of horrendous pain.

Scott and George hit the water hard, but they began to swim immediately, coughing and choking and splashing. Their arms and legs collided with desks and other objects in the water, but they pushed through the darkness that was threatening to swallow them whole. They had no idea which way they were headed, but they knew they had to keep moving. The smoke was smothering, and there was heat above them, as if the ceiling were on fire but producing no light.

They pushed on, side by side, gasping for air and swimming. George was next to Scott, keeping pace—and then suddenly he wasn't.

Scott stopped when he realized George was gone. His feet settled on the floor. The water was up to his chest, but that didn't tell him anything. He stayed very quiet as he listened to the noises echoing around the basement. The smoke wasn't as bad here.

"George?" Scott whispered. "Where the hell are you?"

There was movement to his right and something broke the surface, splashing wildly.

"Help me!" George screamed, his words ending in a wet squeal as he vanished under the water again.

Scott moved blindly toward the splashing and a flailing hand slapped his arm from under the water. He grabbed onto that hand, pulling as hard as he could. He felt the water move as if a heavy weight were being lifted and then he heard coughing and a loud gasp.

"Something pulled me under," George cried, spitting, choking. He didn't wait for Scott to reply and he didn't take a moment to catch his breath. He dove forward and started swimming again.

Scott followed, swiftly catching up. Soon their hands started hitting the floor and they stumbled to their feet and ran, the water sloshing around their knees as they smacked into furniture and equipment, bruising their arms and legs. The pain was tremendous, but they didn't stop.

Although there were still muffled screams and splashing, the smoke was gone and the coldness seemed to be drifting away, too. They still had no idea where they were, but soon the water was only ankle deep, so they had to be headed in the right direction.

They kept running, even though they were running blind,

and without any warning Scott slammed into the maintenance crew's lockers. He howled in pain, the metal edges pushing hard into his flesh. Then George slammed into him, shoving Scott against the metal again, smashing his nose.

"Dammit!" Scott shouted.

"Sorry!" George replied. "I can't see anything!"

"Come on, I know where we are," Scott said, holding his aching nose with one hand and using the lockers as a guide to locate the doorway where they had entered the basement.

Once they found the door again, they rushed up the stairs, climbing them two at a time. Scott heaved the door at the top of the stairs open and stumbled into the hallway, hitting the opposite wall hard and falling backwards. George tripped as he passed through the doorway and landed next to Scott, gasping in short breaths. The door slowly closed behind them.

Scott and George lay there, listening to the storm raging outside and their own heartbeats echoing in their ears. Off in the distance, past the end of the hallway, lightning flashed outside the open loading docks at the far side of the warehouse.

"Jesus H. Christ," Scott said, his breathing heavy. "Let's get the hell out of this hallway and never come back."

They got to their feet and held onto the walls to steady their trembling legs as they walked. They didn't stop moving until they had reached the warehouse and made their way to the open dock doors. Mary was working at the other end of the building and Scott had no idea what he would tell her when she returned.

Lightning flashed, thunder rumbled, and heavy drops of rain spit on Scott's face, but everything about the moment was refreshing to him. Deep down, he felt like he had been born again. He realized he was crying.

"George, I think we're lucky to be alive," Scott said as he watched the storm's fury and wiped the wetness from his face.

When George didn't reply, Scott turned to ask if he was all right, but the words never left his lips.

George stood in the shadows a few feet from the loading dock, his head tilted down and his chin rested on his chest. His thumb flicked at the sparkwheel of a silver lighter—*click, click, click*—until a flame jumped to life in the darkness.

When George's emotionless eyes rose to meet Scott's gaze, Scott wanted to scream but he couldn't. Besides, screaming wouldn't help him now. Screaming wouldn't help at all.

Scott had learned that lesson from the shadowy souls in the smoke, the echoes of the workers whose deaths were seared into the memory of the building. Screaming wouldn't open locked doors, it wouldn't extinguish flames, and it certainly wouldn't stop whatever dreadful horror was about to happen to him.

Scott realized all this and something else even more important:

George had found what they left behind.

CPSIA information can be obtained
at www.ICGtesting.com
Printed in the USA
FSHW020757300319
56712FS